Jack Rabbit Goes To War

BY EARL SNORT

A Jack Rabbit Novel

TotalRecall Publications, Inc.
1103 Middlecreek St.
Friendswood, Texas 77546
281-992-3131 281-482-5390 Fax
www.totalrecallpress.com

ISBN: 978-1-64883-418-9
UPC: 6-43977-44189-8

Library of Congress: 2025944812

FIRST EDITION
1   2   3   4   5   6   7   8   9   10

**Not a speck of this is true.
It's all a figment of my imagination.**

Dedication

This book is dedicated to my wife who has stood by me through thick and thin through all these many years.

It's also dedicated to past colleagues, both military and law enforcement, whose deeds have enriched my books by being woven into the fabric of my stories. This includes JFW who proofs all of my books.

Finally, it is dedicated to my readers who give me feedback. They help me improve future endeavors by letting me know what they liked and what they didn't. It's impossible to be an unbiased critic of your own work.

God Bless America and all those who have done their part to leave a legacy to be proud of for our children and grandchildren and those to follow. Who wants to meet George Washington and Our Founding Fathers in Heaven and tell them we dropped the ball?

"Those were the days my friend.
We thought they'd never end.
We'd sing and dance forever and a day.
We'd live the life we choose.
We'd fight and never lose.
Those were the days.
Oh yes. Those were the days."

Composed by Boris Formin and Gene Raskin and performed by Mary Hopkin in 1968.

Illustrated by Susan C. Barnes.

Preface

An Introduction to the Fantasy Aspect of This Tale

It was a great morning, bright, hot, and sunny in the West Texas hill country. Jack Rabbit was awake, moving away from his burrow, ready for breakfast. He was in the mood for some fresh sprouts and he knew exactly where they were growing up on the hillside. Jack weaved around the cactus and sage brush, starting up the well-known path to higher ground.

After a few minutes he paused, wondering what that sound was. Moving slowly, he hopped closer to see. From behind a giant, red barrel cactus, he nosed around for a peek. To Jack's surprise, an Apache medicine man was chanting and dancing around a small fire. The medicine man was dressed in feathers and his body was painted in many colors. Most noticeable was his left hand. It was painted all white up to his wrist like a glove. In his right hand, he held what appeared to be a ball consisting of stones, sticks, feathers, cloth, and who knows what else wrapped around something which resembled a skull.

Jack heard a small crack and looked up the hillside. A small puff of dust spit out into the sunshine. Jack had seen rock slides before but this was different. He noticed a huge boulder vibrating and beginning to move. He was scared he would be in its path when it came tumbling down. Jack jumped sideways as rabbits do, and bolted. He let out a loud screech, screaming past the dancing medicine man. Shocked out of his trance, the shaman fell backwards into a crevice in the hillside.

Jack had seen the boulder start to fall, so he jumped into the narrow opening to get away from its path. Both Jack and the shaman watched as this very large rock bounced on the trail, falling over the side of the cliff. Without a doubt, Jack had saved the shaman's life.

The shaman looked down at Jack. "Wow! That was close. Thank you for saving my life. What's your name?"

"Jack Rabbit," replied the rabbit.

"Hello, Jack. My name is Mohan. I'm the medicine man for my Apache tribe."

"How do you speak my language?" asked Jack. "How is it I can understand you?"

"My god has empowered me with great wisdom and the ability to perform many wonderous tasks. May I ask you what you desire?"

Jack knew immediately what he wanted. "Currently my life is short compared to yours. I wish to be many things, to go many places, and to have a very long life."

Mohan climbed out of the crevice and rebuilt the fire. Jack remained in the crevice away from danger. Once the fire was just the right size, Mohan returned and went way back, deep into the darkness, mumbling words Jack could not understand. Jack could hear Mohan moving about, tapping and scraping in the dark. Jack jumped when Mohan let out a loud, "Ah ha! Found it!" and shuffled out of the recess. Back to the fire went Mohan, opening his medicine bag along the way. He pulled out several items and began to chant, repeating a rhythmic phrase, and dancing around the fire. After a few minutes, he called for Jack to come out of the crevice.

Cautiously, Jack crept out. He positioned himself close to Mohan, staying away from the cliff side and the fire. He was afraid to get too close to the fire because his fur could burn.

Mohan, still chanting and dancing, threw something into the flames which exploded. Jack jumped farther back, closer to the side of the hill. Mohan laughed and directed Jack to a specific spot. He motioned for Jack to move onto the top of a rock he had placed close to the fire.

Jack was hesitant but decided it would be safe with Mohan. He was nice and had a good voice for chanting.

Mohan stopped suddenly in front of Jack, throwing a dust ball towards him. Jack had been facing Mohan and now both his eyes and ears were filled with powder. In fact, the powder covered Jack from his head all the way down to his lucky feet. Rabbits have lucky feet, you know.

Mohan started to chant and to dance once again. The rhythmic sounds, along with his hypnotic voice, mesmerized Jack, causing him to sway back and forth.

Magical powers swirled all around them. Sparks flew from the fire. Clouds rolled in. Lightning lit up the sky. Rocks crashed down from the hill. Thunder rolled through the valley. Cacti burst into flowers. Grass turned emerald green. Water sprang from the crevice, forming a small creek which pursued gravity down the side of the hill. A star fell. All kinds of strange things happened as Mohan performed his magic spell.

Jack awoke feeling a little strange. Looking around, he saw Mohan sleeping on the ground next to the dying fire. Getting up, Jack hopped down to the creek to get a drink. The water was the sweetest he had ever tasted. Looking some more, he spotted some fresh, green, tender sprouts. They tasted really awesome.

When he was sated, he hopped over to Mohan, who had just begun to rouse.

"What just happened?" asked Jack.

Mohan sat up and stretched. "Well, Jack," he said, "you are now a very special being. You have many powers to experiment with. First, let's test your abilities. Picture in your mind that you are an Apache warrior."

Jack thought, "I am an Apache warrior." The air stood still. A little fire flashed before his eyes. A wind blew in his face, producing a tear.

Mohan said, "Jack, go look at the reflection of your face in the stream."

Moving to the stream, Jack peered into the standing pool and saw an Apache warrior looking back at him. "Mohan," he cried. "What is going on?"

Mohan laughed a little and replied, "Jack, you are now what we call a changeling. A changeling is a being with many powers. Changelings can become anything they wish to be. Also, the spirits have granted you never-ending life. That means you can live forever. In addition, you have the power of time. You can venture to the past or the future; however, there is one catch to this magical existence. You can do no harm to others, except to the bad when they are harming others. Your life is now designed to be helpful to all beings wherever you go. Protect the innocent from the bad. This means you can use force when necessary."

Mohan paused. "Jack, there are two restrictions. You may never visit Easter Island, as the awful 'Z Gods' there will harm you. Also, you may never eat papaya fruit."

Jack wondered, "What is papaya fruit?" He didn't have a clue. Nevertheless, he didn't ask.

Over the next several weeks, Jack changed from one being to another - panther, eagle, mouse, etc. "This is amazing," he thought.

Jack wandered all over Apache territory for many years, changing however he saw fit. He thoroughly enjoyed being a bird. Birds can see many things on the ground in great detail. They fly fast and they travel long distances. He also liked being a ground animal. Being a panther was his favorite. But most of all, Jack liked being human, although he could be a big tree or a small bush when all he wanted to do was watch the world go by.

Jack traveled all over the world through time and space for the next hundred years, getting to experience all kinds of people, places, and things.

This tale is about just one of his adventures - one he especially enjoyed.

Chapter 1
Patriotic Fervor

The year was 1941. John Archibald Rabbit, known by all as Jack, had lived at Rabbit Hollow in Lawrence County, Kentucky, now for 21 human years. He was a moonshiner by profession, and a darn good one, too. He had learned from Cousin Gerard.

Jack had enjoyed this period of his life, but he was getting restless. He had no wife nor children. The only relatives he had in his human life were his sister, Phoebe, a nurse, who lived with her husband, DeLair Aubrey, a pharmacist in Jamestown, North Dakota, and cousin Gerard Silas Twyman, married to Chloe, with their three young'uns right here in Rabbit Hollow, none of whom were changelings, nor did they know he was.

One of Jack's interests had always been reading the newspaper. He liked to keep up with current events. He was especially fascinated by world events, although he resided in the middle of the sticks in southern Appalachia. Call it Nowhere, America. Go figure. He bought a copy of the Louisville *Courier Journal* at least once a week whenever he stopped by Woodrow Falstaff's General Store. The newspapers were never less than two days old by the time he purchased one but that didn't matter to Jack. He read each paper cover to cover before using it as starter for the fireplace and wood burning stove in his one-room cabin, which he and Cousin Gerard built together for him in 1920. Each newspaper he purchased was two cents well spent, and nary a page was ever wasted.

Of major interest over the past two and a half years, were the articles about Nazi Germany trampling her neighbors beginning with Poland, who fell first in 1939, followed by the rest of continental Europe, seizing territory, and enslaving their peoples. This was déjà vu, as if the 20 years since the Armistice were nothing more than a pause for the Germans to rearm and raise a new generation of soldiers, except for one significant difference. This time the Germans served a fanatical dictator named Adolph Hitler (Der Fuhrer) instead of the tyrant King Wilhelm II. It was like 'going from worse to worser' - a lose-lose situation for the German people, although it was doubtful they recognized it while they were plundering most of Europe. It was even a greater loss for her neighbors, who were being enslaved, murdered, raped, and pillaged of literally everything of value.

Jack knew the Germans all too well. He had fought against them during the Great War and had in fact, been severely wounded by their artillery fire. No doubt he would have perished on that fateful day back in 1918 had he been human. All of the other members of his squad did.

Jack read more. The international news kept getting bleaker for the world at large, day by day. Hitler and Nazi Germany were teamed up with the maniacal Fascist Italian Dictator Benito Mussolini (Il Duce), both of whom were intent on conquering North Africa, thus controlling access to the Mediterranean Sea. Il Duce had already conquered Ethiopia, which was a 'weak sister' and no great shakes to boast about, but it 'made his testicles swell up' to the size of cantaloupes by demonstrating to the world just how powerful he and Italy were. This was narcissism at its pinnacle. Ethiopia was a poor, backward country and had no chance of saving itself. Now, Italy and Germany working in concert, were waging war against the British in Egypt, Libya, and Algeria, all of which were located on the southern Mediterranean coast. The newspaper reported that their goal was to seize all the oil fields in North Africa. Jack wondered if that could be true. Was the war in Africa all about oil?

The bad news continued to escalate. The Japanese, under their man-deity Emperor Hirohito, had also been running amok. Japan had already brought the competing fiefdoms within China to their knees, and exploited other weaker, neighboring nations, gobbling up as much of Asia as it could. This was definitely about oil, because Japan was an oil dependent nation and the U.S. had placed an oil embargo on Japan. Now it appeared that Emperor Hirohito was sidling up to Der Fuhrer. This was shocking, because during the Great War, both Italy and Japan had been allies with England, France, Russia, and the U.S. against the Central Powers of Germany, Austro-Hungary, and Turkey.

Had the great world powers traded dancing partners and gone nuts? It would seem so, except the U.S. was not a leading military power. It had largely disarmed since the war. Its armed forces were small, poorly equipped, and in no way prepared for war. The U.S. had isolated itself from the rest of the world, with no appetite to fight European or Asian wars. Leave us the heck alone!

Want even more bad news? Mighty France had already been conquered by the Germans, and England was in dire straits. It seemed as if the entire world except for America was at war. How long could that last before the Americans would be compelled to fight to defend itself?

Jack's thoughts went back to his service in the Great War - 'the war to end all wars'. He had served in the Army for three years, although more than half of that was spent rehabilitating in an Army hospital for injuries sustained in combat. Finally, he was honorably discharged with the rank of private. He never was promoted. Like every other veteran, he had been awarded the Great War Victory Medal. Then several years ago, after the government established medals which had not existed before, he was retroactively awarded a Bronze Star for heroism, and a Purple Heart for injuries sustained in combat. They arrived in the mail one day along with a letter signed by an Army lieutenant colonel assigned to the War Department. It was an unexpected honor, and Jack was proud of them. He put them in his lockbox in his chest with all his other personal treasures, to include the Great War Victory Medal.

Not bad for a rabbit, huh? Jack thought so. Of course, thinking back to those days, his fellow American soldiers were so hungry for fresh meat, had they known he was a rabbit they probably would have tried to kill him for supper. Perish the thought! Eating rabbit is absolutely disgusting! It's like cannibalism!

Time had slowly crept by for Jack while he resided in the Eastern Kentucky backwoods. He was content, making a decent living, and being left alone in peace since the Cincinnati mobsters lost the local moonshine war, but alas! Nothing ever stays the same. One hopes for the best, but sometimes things get worse. This was one of those times - in spades. You can't stick your head in the sand like an ostrich and pretend that everything is going to be okay, because it won't.

Define okay. Being conquered and enslaved to the Germans, Italians, or Japanese? Passively sitting still while the world self-destructs? Give up without taking some initiative to rectify the situation? Live as a free man or a slave? Unfortunately, those are the only two options. Pick your poison. World dominion by fanatical tyrant megalomaniacs was taking place all around America and headed in our direction, like it or not.

'Live free or die!' Death to the tyrants! As the 18th century English philosopher Edwin Burke once observed, "The only thing necessary for the triumph of evil is for good men to do nothing."

After a great deal of consideration, Jack made up his mind. He decided to reenlist in the U.S. Army. On Halloween night, he and his pooch, Oswald, walked over to Cousin Gerard's cabin. They invited him to come in and partake in a sampling of Gerard's newest batch of white lightning, so he did. The kids were out making the rounds of their nearest neighbors' trick or treating - there were only seven houses within two miles - so Gerald and Chloe were making merry with corn liquor. They were already pretty mellow. During the Bonhomme, Jack informed them he was taking the train to Lexington tomorrow to enlist. He asked Gerard to keep an eye out on his property and in his absence, to care for his mule, Alice, and Oswald, his redbone hound.

They thought that was the craziest thing they'd ever heard, and they laughed until they cried. Finally, Cousin Gerard realized Jack was serious.

He asked, "Ain't you a little long in the tooth ta be a sojer boy agin?"

"Yep, but I'm fit and determined to go. If need be, I'll lie about my age. They'll never know the difference. Please, will you all take care of my animals and property until I return?"

"Well of course we will. It goes without askin'. You mind if'n I plant some tobaccy and corn in your fields?"

"I was hoping you would. Thanks to you both."

"Not an issue. How you gettin' ta Louisa ta catch the train?"

"Woodrow said he would take me in his Tin Lizzy. He said he had some business to attend to there anyway - something about buying some more guns and ammo for his inventory since he was getting short. Even he observed that if we do go to war, it'll be nearly impossible to buy firearms or ammo because everything the factories manufacture will go towards the war effort."

(Jack could have transformed himself into a buzzard and flown himself to Louisa just for the fun of it, but his unexplained absence would have created a furor. Likely after he had been missing for a year, the county court would have declared him dead.)

"Dern! You done figgered this all out, ain't cha? I reckon I better stock up on ammo just in case you're right. I'll load up on .30-30s and 16-gauge shells. I'm well fixed with .32s for my Owl Head revolver. Besides, I seldom ever shoot it anymore. I got plenty enough gumption to croak ever' German what trespasses on my land until they finally croak me. You know that."

"I do, but the way things are going, you'll be vastly outnumbered, and they'll turn Chloe and the young'uns into slaves.

"I'll send you all a letter as soon as I can. Count on it."

"Well all righty then. 'Nuff said. Let's have another little taste to wish you well. The young'uns should be back afore long, and they'll kick up a ruckus soon as they know you'll be leaving. We'll miss ya sorely while ye be gone. How long ya think that be?"

"Not sure. I'm signing up for three years. Might end up doing a little more if we wind up in a war. It surely looks like we might be headed in that direction."

"Pshaw! Nobody in America wants ta go ta war agin! Folks just wanta be left alone."

"I agree. What I'm saying is, we might not have a choice. One of those foreign dictators might decide to poke us in the eye with a sharp stick. Then what?"

"Yer right. That would mean war."

After the farewell toast, Jack bade them adieu. He said, "I'll be off before your cock crows in the morning. I'll bring Oswald and Alice over here then. Thank you all once again."

The next morning, Jack met Woodrow at his store. The only things he took with him easily fit into the canvas shoulder bag he was issued during the Great War. They departed at 6:30. Jack caught the 8:15 train to Lexington. He arrived just a little before noon.

He walked to the Armory and met with the Army recruiter. The Navy was there, too. As it turned out, he had no difficulty enlisting, especially after he pulled out his Army discharge papers and three medals. They never prodded him over his age. Ha! Wouldn't they be surprised if he told the truth and said he might be 500 years old? Of course, then they wouldn't have taken him. They'd think he was crazy. Private John A. Rabbit was now serving Day 1 of a new three-year hitch. He sent a telegram to Gerard to inform him.

The following morning, Jack found himself on a train bound to Camp Wheeler, Georgia, which is located near Macon. It took two days because he had three train changes en route. Upon arrival, he was lodged in one of a dozen new replacement barracks pending the commencement of 13 weeks of Infantry

Basic Training. It was scheduled to begin on November 10th.

The dearth of alone time was a major shortcoming in military life which Jack had forgotten all about. It's no small adjustment to learn to live in a densely packed community, especially one with oodles of rules and oversight, and where private time becomes a rare and highly coveted commodity. For example, a soldier sleeps in a bunkbed in a barracks which accommodates at least 40 soldiers on each floor. It's communal living every hour of every single day.

The standard Army barracks floor plan was two rows of two-tiered bunks facing each other with eight feet between bunks, and a 15-foot aisle between the two rows. Some barracks had only one floor, but others had two or three. The cadre in basic training, of which there were two per platoon of 40 recruits, each had a small private room just outside of the common bunk room. It was the same after basic training at one's permanent posting. A private room for a non-commissioned officer (NCO) was a significant luxury the junior troops were not afforded.

Did I mention that the latrines were one-story wooden buildings consisting of a row of eight stools out in the open on one side of the room, and two eight-foot-long horizontal urinals on the other side adjacent to the sinks? At least they had flush toilets! Bathing was accomplished in the other large room. It had hot water and a dozen shower heads and an area to dry off with benches and hooks to change your clothes.

Get with it, dogface! Modesty takes a distant back seat to doing things efficiently at the least possible expense. Get over yourself. In the field, your accommodations will be even more rudimentary. You do remember what bears do in the woods, don't you?

But that's just it! Private time is even more limited during bivouacs and field exercises, whether in basic training or in your permanently assigned unit. Those accommodations include sharing a pup tent with another squad member, usually someone you gee-haw with. That's why soldiers are issued a shelter half. Two halves buttoned together become one pup tent.

The pup tents are just large enough for two soldiers to sleep side-by-side with enough room left over to hold your web gear and rifle. The pup tents are arranged in long, precisely measured rows, precision being a hallmark of the military. They also require a four-inch-deep ditch to be dug (with your issued entrenching tool) all the way around the perimeter to drain rain away from the tent, so everything inside the tent stays dry (relatively speaking).

One can clearly understand then, whether in garrison or in a field setting, a soldier's absence from the ranks is quickly noted. Therefore, the opportunities for Jack to change into a hawk or a fox to do some sightseeing were extremely limited. The years he spent on his farm in Kentucky where he could go where he pleased, when he pleased, and do what he pleased, to include being anything other than his human persona, came crashing down on him like the walls of Jericho. He might have dwelled on this lack of privacy to his psychological detriment, except the troops were kept busy and had very little time to ruminate. If he had a free hour, he usually wrote a letter to Phoebe or Gerard or found some space out of harm's way and enjoyed a cigar in peace.

That being said, Jack did have one blessed opportunity to get some alone time while he was training at Camp Wheeler. He changed into a red-tailed hawk and soared all around the camp.

He could see his current universe. It put everything into perspective. Clearly a lot of planning had gone into the layout. Jack was duly impressed. Everything was precise and neat and tidy.

Free time was drawing short, and he needed to return to the barracks. He didn't want to pay the penalty for being tardy. He began his descent, when he caught the attention of two soldiers he recognized from his company. They were pointing at him like they had never seen a red-tailed hawk before. Probably city slickers. Jack sat down behind a massive sycamore tree out of their sight. He knew they were running over to get a closer look at him, so he quickly changed into a skunk. The moment they rounded the tree, he turned his backside towards them and issued a small spray of the all too unpleasant skunk perfume. They skedaddled unharmed posthaste, leaving Jack to return to his human persona, thus allowing him to fall into ranks just in the nick of time.

Even as a human and not as a changeling, Jack was the oldest man in his company at age 41. He was also the best trainee because he was dedicated, plus he had lots of combat experience. He proudly wore his ribbons whenever they wore Class A (dress) uniforms. Neither of his drill instructors had a Bronze Star Medal or a Purple Heart, so they treated him with more respect than they did for his platoon mates.

A month into training, the diabolical Japanese bombed Pearl Harbor in the Territory of Hawaii, U.S.A. This was the sharp stick in the eye Jack had asked Gerard about. Congress declared war! It added a whole new dimension to their training. Everyone stepped up his performance. The intensity increased tenfold. War was no longer an abstract thought. America was the sleeping dog the Japanese had just kicked. Then the Germans and the Italians piled on and declared war on America, too. Sitting this war out was no longer an option for the United States. Jack had seen it coming for months.

The recruits graduated on February 6th, 1942. Jack was numero uno in his company. He and 11 other new basic training graduates were promoted to Private first class. They sewed a single chevron on the upper sleeves of their uniforms. In addition, Jack had one diagonal service stripe sewn on the bottom of his left sleeve representing three years of previous service, and one short, horizontal stripe sewn on the bottom of his right sleeve, signifying six months of service overseas during the Great War.

During the ceremony, each new graduate was awarded the American Defense Service Medal. President Roosevelt authorized this decoration for all military personnel on active duty with service between September 8, 1939, and December 7, 1941, the day the Japanese bombed Pearl Harbor. (World War II officially began on September 1, 1939, when Germany invaded Poland. Then on September 8, 1939, President Roosevelt declared the U.S. to be in a limited national emergency. Hence the beginning eligibility date for this medal.)

Jack looked at his image in the mirror wearing his winter Class A uniform with his four ribbons on his left chest. His Bronze Star was centered on the top. The Purple Heart, American Defense Service Medal, and Great War Victory Medal were in a row underneath. His Expert Rifleman's badge was centered underneath his ribbons. It was awarded for his proficiency with the Army's new M-1 Garand rifle.

He liked what he saw. He went to a photography shop and had his picture taken for posterity. He purchased three copies - one for Phoebe, one for Gerard, and one for himself. He put the first two in the mail. Now, by gosh, Jack was ready for war!

Chapter 2
Being in Limbo

Pfc (Private first class) John A. Rabbit and 300 other spanking new infantry soldiers were transported by train to Camp Blanding, near Starke, in Clay County, Florida, arriving February 10th, 1942. They all had been assigned to the 1st Division, commanded by a major (two-star) general, forever more reflagged as the 1st Infantry Division, so as not to confuse it with the 1st Armored Division, the 1st Cavalry Division, etc. It was nicknamed The Big Red One for an obvious reason, which they soon came to understand. At Camp Blanding they were issued 1st ID (Infantry Division) patches to sew on the left shoulder of their uniforms. It was a five-sided OD (olive drab) patch with the bottom shaped like a V, and the red numeral 1 in the center; ergo, The Big Red One.

The 1st ID was comprised of three infantry regiments with 3,300 infantrymen each. These were numbered the 16th, 18th, and 26th Infantry Regiments. Division Artillery was comprised of four battalions with 520 artillerymen each. These were numbered the 5th, 7th, 32nd, and 33rd Field Artilleries. In addition, the division had smaller components of battalions and/or a single company of quartermaster (supply), medical, ordnance, engineer, signal (communications), and reconnaissance (scouts). Altogether, the division had 14,000 personnel. It was designed to be self-sustaining. What it did not have was armor (tanks).

It traveled by truck, using 2 ½ ton cargo carriers, called a deuce-and-a-half, which could haul 20 troops. Some staff officers and senior commanders traveled in a small, four-seat general purpose (GP) vehicle, nicknamed a Jeep for obvious reasons. Otherwise, the traditional 'straight-leg' (not airborne) infantry traveled by leather personnel carriers (feet).

Within the 1st Infantry Division, Jack found himself assigned to the 16th Infantry Regiment (commanded by a colonel), 2nd Battalion (commanded by a lieutenant colonel), Able (acronym for A) Company (commanded by a captain), 3rd Platoon (commanded by either a 1st or 2nd lieutenant), 1st Squad (lead by a staff sergeant or a sergeant) as a rifleman. At full strength, the squad was comprised of ten men, including the sergeant, a couple of corporals, and the rest privates first class and privates, the last of which were at the very bottom of the Army hierarchal totem pole. As a member of the squad (MOS) the tongue-in-cheek motto was 'if it moves, salute it.'

Within two days each newbie was issued the venerable M-1 Garand, semi-automatic rifle, which fires 8-round clips of .30-06 ammunition, plus their TA-50 (tactical field gear).

For each soldier, TA-50 included the steel pot (helmet), helmet liner, web pack with shoulder and spaghetti straps (which had to be assembled carefully and painstakingly to fit the individual soldier properly to distribute the weight evenly), bayonet with sheath, web belt (described below) which is fastened to the shoulder and spaghetti straps to hold everything firmly in place, along with other necessary gear.

Other necessary gear included a web belt with ten pouches to hold the 8-round clips of .30-06 ammo, first aid pouch with large, folded cotton bandage, canteen pouch with a stainless steel quart-size canteen inserted inside a stainless steel metal cup with a folding handle for drinking, P-38 (small bi-fold can opener with a hole at the top so you could wear it on the ball chain with your dog tags around your neck so as not to lose it), heavy grade field jacket with liner, wool blanket, mess kit (bi-folding stainless steel, bifurcated dish/plate with folding handle, complete with stainless steel fork, spoon, and butter knife), shelter half, poncho, folding entrenching tool (shovel) with canvas cover (which is attached on the back of the pack), as well as other items as might be necessary.

One example of what might be necessary would be a second canteen and canvas cover for areas where potable water was lacking.

Another might be a compass in a canvas web pouch.

Another for officers might include a leather encased set of binoculars with a strap.

Still yet another might be a leather holster with a flap housing a Government Issue, Model 1911, .45 caliber semi-automatic pistol, manufactured by any of the following companies: Colt, Remington (the typewriter company), Springfield Armory, North American Arms, Ithaca, Union Switch & Signal, and the Singer Sewing Machine Company. All holsters were right-handed and came with a canvas double ammo pouch to hold two spare, 7-shot magazines. Pistols were normally only issued to officers, first sergeants, mortar men, and machine gunners, so Jack didn't have one.

After the troops assembled all their web gear in a satisfactory manner, as determined by the exacting standards set by the Army Field Manual and inspected by their squad leader, platoon sergeant, platoon leader (lieutenant) and company commander (captain), they commenced more training, beginning with a 20-mile forced march loaded down with all field gear. This included an overnight bivouac, followed by a return forced march back to the barracks, usually the next day. This was perhaps the most important training of all. By the time the forced marches were over, every new soldier had his web gear properly assembled to reduce aching shoulders and a sore back, not to mention blisters on his feet if his boots didn't fit properly.

More training followed, to include three weeks on the rifle range, followed by weapons training on the Browning M-2, .50 caliber, belt-fed coaxial machine gun, the M-1918 Browning Automatic Rifle (BAR), .30-06 caliber, with 20-round detachable magazines, and plenty of practice throwing the M-2 pineapple hand grenade, which is the infantryman's best friend in a firefight with closely packed enemy soldiers, especially if they are armed with a machine gun. The heavy weapons platoon also gained a high degree of proficiency with the M-2, 60-millimeter mortar, and the M-1 Bazooka (anti-tank recoilless rocket launcher) with the 60-millimeter M-6 HEAT (high-explosive anti-tank) projectiles.

In June, the troops boarded trains to the Indiantown Gap Military Reservation in Lebanon County, Pennsylvania. The cooler weather was nice. The rank and file didn't have 'the big picture' other than the common understanding that this was all in preparation for combat. Of that, there was no doubt. Although they continued to train hard, because 'idle hands are the devil's workshop' (Proverbs 16: 27-29), unknown to the troops, this move was primarily designed to assemble them for a trans-Atlantic, overseas movement in August.

The rank and file didn't know this either, but the Big Red One had been designated to fight the German Nazis by upper echelon American and British military planners in the opening months of

1941, before the U.S. was even at war! Jack's battalion, the 2nd of the 16th Infantry Regiment, was the advance element of the 1st ID to depart, shipping out on July 31st from the Brooklyn Navy Yard in New York. They arrived in Gourock, Scotland on September 1st, and immediately boarded trains to Tidworth Barracks, near Salisbury, Wiltshire, 50 miles southwest of London, where they were subsequently joined by the rest of the 1st ID.

They trained feverishly, to include one amphibious exercise in Scotland ending on October 18th, immediately after which they embarked on transport ships bound for North Africa. By this time, Jack had been in the Army for almost a year!

Jack wasn't the only soldier who followed the news whenever he could, and he tried to run down any rumor which came his way. By now, in October of 1942, every European nation except for England had capitulated to Germany. France had two governments - the Vichy government who surrendered and served their German masters, and the Free French who were in disarray, essentially stateless and in exile, and fighting with the Allies against the Axis Powers.

London had nearly been bombed into oblivion. In addition, the Germans conquered a huge portion of the British Army, which they drove to the sea at the French port of Dunkirk, which had to be evacuated to preserve the better portion, using every military and civilian ship and dingy available.

Britain probably would have been forced to capitulate, had it not been for President Franklin Delano Roosevelt's Lend-Lease bill. Essentially, the U.S. loaned or leased the British whatever they needed to continue fighting the war from 1940, and ongoing until the bitter end. How's that for helping your neighbor?

Japan was still running amok in all of Asia. The Philippines fell, and U.S. Army General Douglas MacArthur had to be evacuated (against his will). Lieutenant General Jonathan Wainwright and thousands of British and U.S. Army troops were 'left holding the bag' and were either killed, placed into brutal prisoner of war (POW) camps, or went native, fighting in the bush with other displaced allied soldiers and native Filipinos who were waging guerrilla warfare.

The good news was that the U.S. Navy won the aerial and naval Battle of Midway in the Pacific, handing the Imperial Japanese Navy a crippling, although not decisive blow.

Before that though, Army Air Corps Colonel Jimmy Doolittle and a band of derring-do aircrews launched ground-based Army bombers from aircraft carriers, something no one thought could be done, on a one-way flight to bomb the Imperial Japanese Empire. They took off, knowing they couldn't carry enough fuel to return. Nevertheless, most of our airmen evaded capture and survived. Colonel Doolittle received the Congressional Medal of Honor and a promotion to brigadier general.

Of course, that didn't alter the war much because it was just one bombing, but it shamed the warmongering Japanese leaders who thought they were invincible, and it frightened the civilian populace by bringing the war to their doorsteps. It also greatly boosted American morale.

On the flip side of the ledger, about this same time the Japanese Army invaded the Territory of Alaska which went uncontested, and they were still there. So far, the Japs hadn't made much headway on U.S. soil, but still it was alarming and had to be dealt with soon.

From the very beginning and throughout all their training, the troops in the 1st Infantry Division universally thought they would be fighting in Nazi Germany, or at least in France. Now they knew otherwise. They were headed for Africa.

Most of them had heard of German Field Marshal Erwin Rommel and his Afrika Korps, maybe even saw news clips of him and his panzers in movie newsreels, but they had no idea why he and the Italians were fighting in North Africa against the Brits and their satellite allied countries, to include Australia, New Zealand, India, South Africa, Free French, Greek, and the Libyan Arab Force. North Africa was nothing more than an enormous, barren sandbox at least as big as the state of Texas, maybe more (and probably even hotter.) Not only that, but they had also not known all these other countries were even involved. Of course, the strategic reason was the Axis Powers wanted to seize the oil fields, but that wasn't readily apparent to Private Joe Bag o' Doughnuts, especially if he grew up in a moderate climate with hardwood trees, creeks, pastureland, and rivers. For soldiers like Private Joe Bag o' Doughnuts, North Africa was the closest thing to Hell he'd ever experienced, even before bullets were zinging past his head.

On the way to Africa, they learned that the Axis (Germans, Italians, and Vichy French) had been engaged against the Allies (and everyone else mentioned in the previous paragraph) for more than two years. It was a seesaw affair, with the Allies having just won a major victory against the Axis Powers, specifically the Germans and Italians (since the Japanese remained in Asia) at the Second Battle of El Alamein in Egypt. (The first battle there had been a stalemate.)

Egypt is located on the southern shore of the Mediterranean Sea in the northeast corner of the African continent. The Americans, as the 'new kids on the block', and specifically the Big

Red One, were enroute to join their allied brethren to finish them off in a campaign named Operation Torch. None other than General Dwight D. Eisenhower was in overall command! That was a huge morale builder to several divisions of U.S. soldiers, in which very few had ever experienced combat. It was also significant because the British had very little respect for the Americans' fighting prowess since they were nearly all green troops. In fact, they derisively referred to the Americans as 'Colonials'. The Brits were soon to learn otherwise.

It was all coming to a head for Jack and the 1st Infantry Division.

Chapter 3
Shots Fired - Getting Blooded

Jack knew the invasion force was divided into three separate groups. The 1st Division was in the Center Task Force, which was all he really cared about. (You know - one tidbit at a time for the lowly rifleman.) It was an all-American force commanded by Major General L. Fredendall, whom he'd never seen nor even heard mentioned before; however, he had 'laid eyes' on the Big Red One Division Commander, Major General Terry Allen. Ditto for Colonel Truman K. Borders, a West Point graduate, Class of 1926, and commander of the 16th Regiment, to which Jack was assigned. Same-same for Lieutenant Colonel Randall T. Lee, Stanford ROTC, Class of 1932, commander of 2nd Battalion, also to which Jack was assigned.

The Central Task Force had 39,000 troops, consisting of the 1st Infantry Division, the 1st Armored Division, and a complement of U.S. Army Rangers, who were the toughest soldiers in the U.S. Army. The mission was to capture Oran in Algeria. They were escorted there courtesy of the British Navy.

For the record, the Western Task Force had 35,000 soldiers and was commanded by Major General George S. Patton. It was also an all-American force, consisting of the 3rd Infantry Division, 2nd Armored Division, and most of the 9th Infantry Division. The mission was to capture Casablanca in Morocco and then assist the Center Task Force. They were transported by a U.S. Navy flotilla commanded by Rear Admiral H.K. Hewitt.

Finally, the Eastern Task Force was a mixed bag, consisting of

23,000 British infantry and commandos, and 10,000 U.S. soldiers from the 34th Infantry Division, which was commanded by Major General Charles Ryder. Truly, the Eastern Task Force was commanded by British Vice Admiral Sir Harold Burrough, but General Ryder was named as the overall commander for political reasons. The French held a grudge against the British for sinking their warships in the Mediterranean after the Germans overran France and created the Vichy government. The British had been afraid the French Navy would turn against them, and for good reason. The 'proof in the pudding' was that the Vichy French Army was fighting against the British here in Africa. The Eastern Task Force mission was to capture Algiers in Algeria.

The Center Task Force arrived on November 7th. They landed at Les Andalouses, west of Oran and east of Arzew. They expected to fight Germans but were shocked to be fighting the Vichy French. This was incomprehensible! Nevertheless, for the 1st Infantry Division as a whole, the fighting was sporadic, the reason being that some Vichy fought ferociously while others were lackadaisical. Those fighting against the battalion Pfc Rabbit was assigned to, the 2nd Battalion, 16th Infantry Regiment, fought tenaciously.

For Able Company, 2nd Battalion, war began in earnest on November 9th. The 1st Infantry Division's mission was to capture Oran, and they set out to do it. Each regiment, battalion, and company had its marching orders.

The 2nd Battalion soon learned to ignore that they were fighting the French instead of the Germans. Bullets are bullets. They slay friends and foes alike without regard. 2nd Battalion got down to business and killed as many Vichy French combatants as they could. If the Vichy French, whom they euphemistically called Frogs, didn't throw up a white flag and drop their weapons, they would send them straight to Heaven or to Hell, whichever was appropriate for each departed soul.

Able Company's 3rd Platoon, to which Jack was assigned, was led by Southern Mississippi College and OCS (Officer Candidate School) graduate 2nd Lieutenant Hugh C. Greeley, Jr. of Gulfport, Mississippi. He was a 'kick butt and take names' kind of guy. The term gung-ho applied.

Lieutenant Greeley was tasked by Able Company Captain 'Diamond Jim' Brady Carr, an Ole Miss ROTC grad from Maury County, Tennessee, to knock out a machine gun emplacement which was holding up the advance. It was located at the top of a bluff with a hidden ravine, which also sheltered what was believed to be a squad-size element of soldiers which was also laying down heavy fire. Not having armor available at the time, Lieutenant Greeley decided on a frontal attack. He led the charge, rallying his entire platoon. This was 3rd Platoon's collective baptism under fire.

1st Squad, including Jack, led by Staff Sergeant Albert S. Cain of Lake Charles, Louisiana, was at the forefront of the attack. Ever heard of the Rebel yell? If not, you would have learned all about it here. They used whatever kind of cover was available, which wasn't much unless you counted anthills. They encountered a hundred yards of flying lead in their effort to breech the emplacement.

Halfway there, Jack kneeled and took aim at the enemy soldier he could see very well, who was feeding the belt of ammunition into the machine gun which was pinning them down. Jack drilled him in his left side with three well-placed shots, which caused a momentary lapse in machine gun fire.

That's all the 3rd Platoon needed. By then, Lieutenant Greeley, who was closest to the emplacement, shot the machine gunner dead. This was immediately followed up by the rest of the platoon, which swarmed the ravine and mowed down the entire group of enemy riflemen. They killed 23 altogether. Not one Vichy French soldier was left alive, and no one in the 2nd Battalion was the least bit sorry.

3rd Platoon had two casualties. Private Ralph F. Goodfellow from Lincoln, Nebraska was killed with a shot through his heart. Private first-class Dennis G. Byrd from Beaumont, Texas, was wounded in his right thigh. He was treated in the MASH (Mobile Army Surgical Hospital) and returned to the unit two weeks later.

Also, weeks later after the dust had settled, awards were passed out. Lieutenant Greeley received a Bronze Star Medal for Valor. Private first-class John A. Rabbit received an Army Commendation Medal. Private first-class Dennis Byrd and Private Ralph Goodfellow were awarded a Purple Heart. The latter's was awarded posthumously.

The following day, the Center Task Force captured Oran. It certainly helped that Admiral Francois Darlan, high commissioner for the Vichy government, surrendered unconditionally. On November 10th, he signed an armistice with the Allies. Now the former Vichy French units in North Africa became part of the Allies. Operation Torch was technically over, and they entered into a new, unnamed phase of combat.

The 1st Infantry Division continued an uneventful steady advance towards the Tunis front. Then in late November, the division was broken up into battalion-strength units and combined with various other American and British elements. Only the higher-ups had 'the big picture' and knew why.

Generally speaking, 2nd Battalion continued its advance with only minor, sporadic skirmishes against outlier German and Italian forces, all of which were resolved decisively in 2nd Battalion's favor.

Whenever Able Company was stationary for a day or two and nobody was paying attention, Jack transformed himself into a hawk to try to figure out which units were where. For the most part, other than being able to discern which units were American or British or German or Italian, he picked up very little useful intelligence. Not only that, landing and reverting into Jack the soldier was extremely problematic. That's because it was difficult finding an isolated spot near his company without being seen or shot by a nervous sentry.

November morphed into December and December morphed into January. Nobody in Able Company had yet to fire a shot in anger at either the Germans or the Italians during this unnamed mission, although plenty of other American units, including 1st Infantry Division's 18th Regiment, 26th Regiment, and 33rd Field Artillery had.

In mid-January, the 1st Infantry Division was finally reunited in Southern Tunisia near Guelma, which was 60 miles east of Constantine. Guess what happened then. Before the month had ended, the division was once again broken up into battalion and company-size units and committed to action separately over a 200-mile expanse of desert extending from Medjez el Bab to the north, through the Ousseltia River Valley in the center, to Gafsa in the south.

Jack lost track of time and dates because Able Company stayed on the move and had been engaged in a series of skirmishes with small elements of Rommel's Afrika Korps. Heck!

It was all he could do to keep up with 3rd Platoon's combat action. Suffice it to say, by the time the division was reunited in the middle of February, Able Company had suffered eight new casualties, to include two killed. By the grace of God, none were from 3rd Platoon. The good news was that now each soldier in 2nd Battalion had experienced combat and was learning from his mistakes. The green recruits from November 9th were now weather-beaten, dirty, and beginning to get a little salty. So far, so good. They had yet to experience overwhelming odds.

In each of these engagements, Jack kept his head down and tried to make each of his shots count. It was nearly impossible in the middle of the night to hit the 10-ring unless they had a full moon. Of course, the moon shared its light with both sides. Besides that, Jack wasn't pressing for a rack full of medals. He already had plenty. His goal was simple - to kill as many of the enemy as he could while saving his own life and the lives of his compatriots. End of statement.

It seemed like Jack had hardly finished these ruminations when Captain Carr addressed the company, holding a corrugated cardboard box full of smaller blue cardboard boxes under his arm. Each of the enlisted soldiers with more than one year of active duty during wartime had been awarded the Good Conduct Medal. During peacetime, the criteria required three years of good behavior. This decoration was something relatively new. The Army only authorized it in 1941, when America's war began. The Navy had been issuing them since the 1880s. Ditto for the Marines. Go figure.

Jack put it in his pack, hoping it wouldn't get damaged before he could put it with his others which were stored in his duffle bag. Then he wondered. Where did the Army put all their duffle bags after they offloaded at Les Andalouses?

On February 14ᵗʰ, things began to heat up again. Nearly all of the 1ˢᵗ Infantry Division was still in the Ousseltia River Valley but scattered along 200 miles of rough terrain. On that day, the Big Red One learned that General Hans Jürgen von Arnim's 5ᵗʰ Panzer Division had launched an assault at Faid Pass, 80 miles south of the Ousseltia River Valley. The 1ˢᵗ Armored Division had been chewed up pretty badly. In addition, Field Marshal Erwin Rommel's Panzer Division captured Gafsa, and was pushing north to combine with the 5ᵗʰ Panzer Division at the Kasserine Pass.

On February 16ᵗʰ, the 1ˢᵗ Infantry Division was ordered to withdraw from the river valley and skedaddle to the Kasserine Pass posthaste. This was an audacious order, which mandated a frenetic push for the division to get there before it was too late, but late they were. 'Close, but no cigar.'

Jack and his comrades were thankful they didn't have to walk all that way; however, a six-day rollercoaster ride bouncing around in the back of a hell-bound deuce-and-a-half, the Army's 2 ½ ton truck with wooden rail bench seats on both sides, each of which holds ten cramped soldiers facing each other with all their combat gear, protected from rain (ha!) under a canvas tarp, on rocky dirt roads was no picnic in the park. It was tortuous. Ya think? Any volunteers?

The Germans arrived on February 19ᵗʰ and attacked on the 20ᵗʰ. The British armor and infantry, assisted by an artillery battalion from the U.S. 9ᵗʰ Infantry Division, drove the Germans back. On February 23ʳᵈ, the Germans withdrew.

'No rest for the weary and the wicked don't need none' but boy were they pleasantly surprised! The 1ˢᵗ Infantry Division was subsequently dispatched to Morsott, northwest of the Tébessa Province in northern Algeria to regroup. They were given a 10-day rest. 'Never look a gift horse in the mouth' but there was nothing to see there and nothing to do.

Quit your bellyaching, dogface. 'You got it made in the shade.' 'Some guys would complain if they were hung with a new rope.' Are you one of them? Be happy.

Maybe doing nothing was the big idea. They'd been in a combat zone for four months, dodging bullets, doing their best to destroy the enemy, seeing friends die or get wounded, eating cold C-rations, drinking nasty alkali water with halazone purification tablets to prevent sickness or death from tainted water, and functioning on very little sleep. Rest is what they needed, plus showers, new clean uniforms and boots, hot food, and nobody belting out anything other than the most essential of orders.

This was time to let your bowels and digestive tract return to normal; tend to your minor injuries - blisters, scratches, cuts, burns, rashes, bug bites, and other aggravating ailments which had been left unattended; catch up on lost sleep; write letters; read your issued New Testament; completely satisfy your tobacco habit if you had one (and most of the combat soldiers did); abstain from alcohol in this Muslim country (bummer); play cards; clean your weapons; replenish commodities for your pack; sharpen your bayonet; purchase souvenir items from the natives; gamble on bug races; josh around with your buddies; contemplate your navel; and then, prepare to go back to war.

Wasn't that your big idea anyway? Fight for your nation. Vanquish the enemy. Don't you remember how a grateful nation honored the doughboys in their uniforms when they returned from the Great War? Remember the parades and flags and all the well-wishers? Beautiful women rushing up to kiss the heroes. That will be you. All you have to do is what you're told and come back in one piece. Got it? Yeah, right. Easier said than done.

Simple, right? KISS - Keep It Simple, Stupid. The Army mantra. One step at a time. Don't get ahead of yourself. Don't dwell on disturbing events. Don't lose perspective. You're making a difference. Someday when you're an old man everything you did here will come together. You and everyone in your family will be proud you served. You are one link in that long line of patriots, stretching all the way from Bunker Hill in the Revolutionary War to here in Morsott, Algeria. You are a proud American fighting man. Never lose sight of that.

Jack managed to sneak off on several occasions to soar like an eagle. He wanted to swim like a porpoise in the Mediterranean Sea, but it was 200 miles away. He couldn't get away for that long. However, his private time flying up high above the land as a bird of prey was soothing to his soul. It was too bad his fellow soldiers couldn't do this also. It greatly enhanced his attitude about life. He was a better person upon his return.

'All good things come to an end.'

Time to go. Gear up. Move out.

Chapter 4
More Combat

The Big Red One in its entirety was deployed to attack the Italians at Gafsa, which was captured by Rommel a month before. He turned it over to the Italians. Surprise. Surprise. The Italians must have seen them coming because they 'took a powder'. Nobody home. Adiós amigo. They forfeited the game. Gafsa was captured on March 17th without a shot being fired in anger. No problem. The 1st Infantry Division planted its flag in a manner of speaking and began sending out patrols to locate the vanishing Italians. It didn't take long. The Recon boys made contact just east of Guettar.

On March 20th, the division attacked with 'all hands-on deck'. A full-scale battle ensued. Jack's perspective was limited to what little he could see of Able Company, but mostly from what he and other members of his squad and platoon did. This was 'the fog of war'. Only the senior commanders knew where the division as a whole was advancing, and where it was not.

For Jack, this was pretty much a textbook battle of run, cover, fire, and maneuver with an enemy who was falling back. Able Company trucks brought the troops up to the front as far as they could go without sustaining enemy fire. Then the troops disembarked and traveled by LPCs (leather personnel carriers). As soon as the 3rd Platoon neutralized the area right in front of them, they moved forward and did it again, and again, and again. It was exhilarating because the enemy appeared to be afraid of them and was attempting to escape. Jack downed nine Eye-Ties

(Italians) during the first two skirmishes. Transformed them into buzzard food. 3rd Platoon was 'mopping up' just like Superman crushing villains in the comic strips, at least as far as Jack could tell. If only war could always be this favorable . . . .

By dusk, at least in the 3rd Platoon's sector, the enemy had retreated nearly five miles to their rear. Surprise. They cut and ran from the Colonials. The battalion commander had called a halt for the night. It was well received by the troops, who were worn out and hungry. They had burned at least 4,000 calories today, as they did most days when they were engaged in combat.

The motor transports came up from the rear, bringing water, ammo, and food. The food consisted of boxed C-rations, which they heated in their mess kits with a Size A (small) 1.25-ounce, Fuel Tablet, Ration Heating, as the military labeled it, when they were available, which was not always the case. Tonight they were, which brought smiles to everyone. One little tablet provided enough heat for one meal, which always tasted better hot.

Tonight, Jack's meal consisted of canned lima beans with (very little) pork. Jack liked lima beans, and heated they tasted just fine. The cardboard box of 'C-rats' also contained a packet of peanut butter and crackers, tiny packets of salt, pepper, and sugar, packet of halazone water purification tablets, packet of instant coffee, canned peaches in heavy syrup, a four-pack of cigarettes (Old Gold this time), packet of waterproof matches, packet of folded toilet paper, packet of sweetened cocoa powder, and a small, hard, waxy bar of chocolate. Jack was famished, so he ate and drank it all except for the cigarettes which he saved for an emergency in the event he ran out of his stash of Certified Bond Blunts (cigars), before he returned to civilization.

Jack expected more of the same manner of warfare on the following day, but he and the rest of his junior-enlisted buddies had an unwelcome surprise. Indeed. Overnight, the Germans and their panzers came to the Eye-Tie's rescue. The Big Red One had no armor, so it was primarily up to the four field artillery battalions and the heavy weapons platoons with their bazookas and heavy mortars to save the day. In between bouts of earth-shattering pounding from both sides, there were sporadic maneuvering firefights between the opposing infantry riflemen.

Then on April 7th, after days of heavy fighting by the big guns on each side, the Germans and Italians broke off and withdrew. Jack wondered if it was because they had finally run out of tank ammo. He certainly hoped so. He didn't care where they went, just so long as they didn't come back.

It's a pretty lopsided fight between a rifleman and a tank. The tank can blow down buildings with its 'tube' (cannon) and crush emplacements with its treads. It also has a machine gun in the front, also shielded by its armor. If the rifleman didn't possess a satchel charge, (a leather satchel with a shoulder strap filled with dynamite and two priming assemblies, usually only issued to combat engineers), his only means of defense was to climb up on the tank from the rear (if it's buttoned up), open the hatch, drop a primed pineapple grenade inside, close it up, and run for the hills.

After a week of recuperating, 'licking its wounds', and replenishing supplies, the Big Red One trucked 150 miles north to the vicinity of Béjaïa, Algeria, a coastal city on the Mediterranean Sea. The mission was simple in concept. Clear the Tine River Valley and its flanking hillsides for the final push to Tunis, which is located on the northernmost tip of Tunisia abutting the coast on the Mediterranean Sea.

It was a difficult mission. The terrain was rugged, and the defenders owned the high ground. The Big Red One launched on April 22nd and continued their push in a northeasterly direction towards Tunis, sustaining many casualties along the way. 3rd Platoon had six KIA (killed in action) and eight WIA (wounded in action). 1st Squad suffered two each of those, all good guys.

It seemed that Jack, besides being a changeling, had a 'lucky charm' in his pocket. He came out unscathed in the midst of all that combat, although he did have two close calls. One time he was hit in the chest by a spent bullet (ricochet) which brought him down like a cadaver, knocking the wind out of his chest for which he sustained a long-lasting bruise.

The other time as he crested a hill, an enemy German soldier pulled the trigger at him point blank. Thankfully, his rifle jammed. Jack ran him through with his bayonet, gizzard to Adam's apple, and then shot two of his companions dead, not stopping until his 8-round clip was empty. Fear causes you to react in ways you never would have considered possible. Jack already had a Purple Heart from the Great War. He didn't cotton to the idea of getting another. The first one was a bad enough experience and had cost him a year-and-a-half of his life recuperating.

Then good fortune showed up on May 13th. Combat concluded before they had completed their push. That was the day the Axis forces threw up the white flag in Tunis. It brought an end to all the fighting in North Africa. The War moved to Italy.

The 1st Infantry Division was ordered back to a training camp in Arzew, Algeria, which is also located on the coast of the Mediterranean Sea. Thankfully, the Army quartermasters had already brought the division duffle bags over from Les

Andalouses and deposited them there at Arzew. What a morale booster! However, at the same time this clearly confirmed that the rear echelon, the 'ash and trash', also known as 'shoe clerks', knew more about what was going on in the war than the dogfaces actually fighting it. Sheesh!

While they were standing down, all U.S. military personnel in North Africa received the European-African-Middle Eastern Campaign Medal, abbreviated as EAME. For those in the Big Red One, they were also awarded three campaign stars - one each for campaigns in Egypt-Libya, Algeria-French Morocco, and Tunisia - to pin on that ribbon. They didn't know it yet, but they would receive others. They also received the Arrowhead device for their amphibious landing at Les Andalouses, which was also pinned on the EAME to the left of all the campaign stars. The arrowhead was held in high esteem by all servicemen who knew what it represented. Amphibious landings nearly always result in incredible losses of killed and wounded.

Then the infantrymen received the most prestigious decoration of all. They were awarded the coveted Combat Infantryman Badge (CIB), an award worn above all their ribbons. In the Army, only the Congressional Medal of Honor is higher.

Jack's 'rack' was expanding. All awards were worn on the left breast above the pocket. The CIB was at the very top above all the rest. Below that, he had a row of one with just his Bronze Star centered below the CIB. The second row had his Army Commendation Medal, Purple Heart, and Good Conduct Medal. The third row had his American Service Defense Medal, EAME, and his Great War (now called World War I) Victory Medal. That was a whole lot more 'egg salad' than he had ever expected to earn.

They all wondered what was next on the horizon. The Big Red One had suffered a lot of casualties and needed scores of replacements if they were to continue fighting. Apparently, the higher-ups had already come to that conclusion, but before the replacements arrived the attrition resulted in a lot of promotions, to include one for Jack.

He was now Corporal John A. Rabbit, United States Army, standing on the bottom rung of the NCO (non-commissioned officer) ladder. Now he had authority over those soldiers in the lower grades, which for Jack meant private and private first class. They were often referred to as the EMs (enlisted men, even though many were draftees). It was a big step up for Jack. Imagine that - corporal in a year-and a-half! Wait until Phoebe and Gerard learn about this. He quickly dashed off a letter to both.

They rested, ate well, received replacement clothing, boots, and other necessary items which had been lost in combat or had worn out. As an NCO, Jack received a compass and spent two weeks in training learning how to use it properly, especially in conjunction with a 1:25,000 topographical map. As an NCO, he was expected to be able to successfully lead squad-size patrols 'in the bush'. It was a heady responsibility, and you better not get lost.

The replacements arrived en mass. The 3rd Platoon received eight. Some of the old hands wouldn't 'give them the time of day'. Jack thought that was nonsense. He treated them all like he wanted to be treated - with respect. He'd 'been in their shoes' in both wars. He'd been scared just like they were. Heck! He was still scared when the bombs and bullets were flying. He hoped the old vets would come around, and most did.

They commenced training hard. The newbies were put through the paces to catch them up. It was difficult for them, especially when they were shoulder-to-shoulder with old hands who made it hard for them for no good reason. Jack knew they needed these newbies to be successful in future combat missions so everyone would come out alive.

During their free time, they pondered their near future. They could tell that something was afoot. The officers and senior NCOs attended numerous meetings, but nobody was sharing. They 'let the cat out of the bag' in July.

Chapter 5
Sicily

On July 4th, the 1st Infantry Division was still standing down in Arzew, Algeria. The unit was treated to a surprise celebration, but no fireworks. Most of the troops had already experienced what the fireworks actually represent. They could live without it. What they did have was an 'all hands-on deck' formation, with a brief rah rah speech by their commander, Major General Terry de la Mesa Allen, Sr., commending them on their outstanding performance and dedication to duty.

It began with a prayer by the Division Chaplain, Lieutenant Colonel Eugene F. Roundtree. Everyone knew his story. He was a 1st Division legend. He enlisted in the Army upon graduation from Vanderbilt University in Tennessee. President Woodrow Wilson had just proclaimed the 'call to arms' signaling America's entry into the Great War, which was in its third year at the time. In the 2nd Battle of the Marne, the young Corporal Roundtree single-handedly attacked a German machine gun nest, killing all within it, thus saving the lives of the men in his platoon who were pinned down. After the war, he was awarded a Distinguished Service Cross for his valor.

Upon receiving his honorable discharge from the Army, he enrolled as a seminarian at Princeton College in New Jersey. Upon graduation and ordination as a Presbyterian minister, he returned to the Army as a chaplain. He now had more than 20 years of service. He was a kind, gracious man, and revered by all the troops in the Big Red One.

Next, Major General Terry gave a short but rousing speech. He commended their service in North Africa. He cited their accomplishments and thanked them all. He said they were in for a real treat, which was the biggest Top Secret he'd ever had to keep in his whole life. He said, "You'll see." Then he buttoned his lip and stepped down from the platform.

Next, the Division Band played the Star-Spangled Banner, America the Beautiful, patriotic marching songs by John Philip Sousa, and concluded with Dixie. This fired everyone up, all proud to be an American.

Then they disassembled and had an old-fashioned hamburger and weenie roast. It was all you could eat, including potato salad, coleslaw, fresh tomatoes, melons of all types, potato chips, pretzels, both sweet and dill pickles, and apple pie. No ice cream. Not enough ice. Still, it was a nice spread. It brought back fond memories of home and days gone by to nearly everyone. In that regard, it made more than one soldier homesick, generating a flurry of letter writing activity.

Then came the biggest surprise ever - the Top Secret. Somehow, General Terry got his hands on a boatload of Oertel's '92 beer which an anonymous patriotic benefactor had donated. Rumor had it, the donor was the owner of the brewery, John F. Oertle himself, who had served as a colonel from the activated Kentucky militia and fought in the Great War. Allegedly, he and Major General Terry were old friends. He donated the beer to give something back to the 'doughboys' of World War II. It was an astonishing gift, as in 2,000 cases of 12-ounce longnecks! They didn't have enough ice to keep it chilled, but after the first few sips, who cared? Everyone except for the lushes had all they wanted.

At the end of the day, all the empty bottles were placed back into the cases. Once again, the quartermaster boys came through. They loaded all the cases onto trucks and managed to return them to the freighter from which they arrived. Everyone else in the division 'policed the area' and except for the occasional pile of vomit, a person would never have known they'd had a beer party, especially a Muslim person.

Jack and his pals were all in a good mood when they fell into a reveille breakfast formation the next morning. After a filling meal of pancakes, maple syrup, pork patty sausage, milk, coffee, and orange juice, they once again assembled in formation. This time it was brief and sobering. Major General Terry informed everyone in the division they were headed back into combat, and they were leaving today. They had until 1400 hours to get ready. He said each respective regiment, battalion, and company commander would brief his command. Then he wished them all well.

The new mission was called Operation Husky. It included a cast of more than a hundred thousand soldiers and sailors on the Allied side. Specifically, it was comprised of British Field Marshal Bernard Montgomery's 8th Army, the American 7th Army, commanded by Lieutenant General George S. Patton, Jr., and Lieutenant General Omar N. Bradley's II Corps, to which 1st Infantry Division was a subordinate unit.

This was as big as Operation Torch! They all knew something was coming but had no idea what. Now all was about to be revealed.

The target was Sicily, meaning that this was another amphibious invasion, ultimately replete with a second arrowhead device and another tiny bronze star to pin on their

EAME medals, whether or not they survived this mission.

Dern! Amphibious landings were dangerous, and especially so if the landing were contested. The planners always had to assign far more troops than necessary to accomplish the mission because many would become casualties before they even set foot on shore. Not only that, but weren't the Marines supposed to be the amphibious landing experts? If so, how come they sent all the Gyrenes to the Pacific?

Jack shrugged. No guts. No glory. Suck it up, dogface. 'Theirs not to reason why. Theirs but to do and die.' Brave and lofty words penned by the poet Lord Alfred Tennyson, who back in 1854 was not a combatant in the suicidal *Charge of the Light Brigade.*

Even though Jack knew as a changeling he would live 'til eternity (supposedly), he still had a really bad feeling about this mission. This time he felt like a mortal. He had a premonition that something really bad was going to happen to him. Did he believe in premonitions? He wasn't sure, but whatever this feeling was, it sure was unsettling.

He wondered. Living forever doesn't necessarily mean you will not be blind, or you will have all your limbs, does it? He'd never considered that before. Now for the first time since Jack had become a changeling, he had the same pit in his stomach, the same butterflies, the same urge to wretch, as all his fellow soldiers who were gearing up for battle. Jack was spooked.

He shook it off and got busy. He checked by the trash cans outside the mess hall, retrieving a corrugated cardboard box suitable for mailing. Once upon a time, it held a dozen 16-ounce jars of Vermont maple syrup. He repurposed it to ship all his military awards and precious documents addressed to himself,

Corporal John A. Rabbit, c/o Mr. Gerard S. Twyman, Rabbit Hollow, Lawrence County, Kentucky. He also enclosed a letter in which he asked Gerard to store these important items until he returned home. He dropped it off at the Army Post Office (APO) before running down to the Post Exchange (PX), where he purchased a dozen five-packs of Certified Bond cigars. Actually, he bought all they had on display. He had no idea when he might have the opportunity to purchase some more.

Then he returned to his temporary housing, which he shared with squad mates in a GP (General Purpose) Medium tent. He prepared all his military gear for deployment, neatly folding everything he couldn't take, and stuffing it into his duffle bag for storage, where he knew not, but he'd bet a dollar to a doughnut hole that the quartermaster boys already knew where.

That evening they boarded transport ships - LSTs, the official Navy acronym for Landing Ship, Tank, but known as Large Slow Targets by the sailors who crewed them. The LSTs have a blunt flat bow which can be lowered when they approach the shore to allow tracked vehicles or troops to disembark. The flat bow makes the vessel difficult to navigate and creates a choppy ride even without crashing waves. LSTs can carry up to 18 Sherman tanks or 160 soldiers. (Most armor companies have 18 tanks, and most infantry companies have 160 soldiers.)

They boarded in Tunisia and embarked for Gela, which is located along the coast of Sicily. The transit was uneventful until the evening of July 9th, when they encountered strong winds, meaning choppy seas. Many men got seasick. Fortunately, Jack did not. That was the extent of the good fortune, at least as it applied to Jack.

The bad fortune, more aptly called misfortune, which applied to all the invaders was that the Army planners had expected to make a surprise landing, so they did not ask for naval pre-invasion bombardment to soften up enemy emplacements. Furthermore, air support was lacking and/or non-existent for the first 36 hours. Worst yet, the enemy knew they were coming and was fully prepared to contest the landing with scores of bombers and fighters, not to mention three major coastal artillery emplacements situated on the bluffs a half mile or so from the shoreline. Furthermore, they had machine gun emplacements all across the landing area. From Private Joe Bag o' Doughnuts' perspective, this was a soup sandwich - a veritable goat rope. It was poorly planned and as a result, poorly executed.

The invasion flotilla began heading for shore at 0100 hours on July 10th. They were still six miles out at sea. Almost immediately, the enemy coastal artillery batteries opened up on them. In addition, scores of sorties by enemy fighters and bombers swarmed like hornets. This wasn't survival of the fittest. This was survival of the luckiest. No Navy or Army fighters showed up to challenge the enemy planes or chase them off! It was as they say, 'like shooting fish in a barrel'.

Jack knew the Big Red One was assigned to Task Force H. He also knew that the division's first objective was to capture the Ponte Olivo Airfield. The 16th Regiment, 2nd Battalion was supposed to attack the city of Gela located on the high ground, following close on the heels of a battalion of Army Rangers.

Jack and everyone else present watched in shock and awe as several of the Navy warships were blown out of the water, not to mention a number of loaded LSTs. Fortunately for Able Company, to include Jack, their LST was not hit. Their LST stopped as planned, 100 yards or more from the shoreline. The front gate dropped, and the troops fully encumbered with gear, began fast-stepping down the ramp into three feet of rolling waves. The bombing and artillery and machine gun fire was incessant. Onward they went. Death surrounded them. There was no other choice. There was nowhere to hide. Gotta make land to fight back to have a chance to survive.

The sand was exceedingly soft and squishy. Jack had difficulty wading through it. It was overcast and dark, except for the explosions of artillery fire and the flashes of staccato machine gun riffs. Add to that, bombs falling from the sky and strafing by the fighters. Soldiers were dropping like horse turds, soon lost to sight in the murky, pounding waves, but very quick to make their appearances known when you tripped on one.

Jack tried to follow Platoon Sergeant Donn Adams and his platoon leader, 2nd Lieutenant Hugh Greeley, but in the mass confusion he lost sight of both.

Suddenly, it was lights out for Jack. He was hit on the head by a machine gun bullet. It was a glancing blow, searing a gash along the left side of his steel pot and helmet liner, slicing the side of his temple for four inches just above his ear. Jack had cinched up the chin strap real tight prior to disembarking so he wouldn't lose his helmet, and although it was twisted sideways to the right due to the impact of the bullet, it didn't fall off although Jack didn't realize it at the time. He was knocked unconscious and fell backwards into the water like dozens of other soldiers before and after him.

The difference was, Jack was sucked into a four-foot cavern under the water with the weight of his gear acting like a boat anchor and planting him on the bottom, six or seven feet below the surface. He was lost to all but did not become one of the bloated corpses washing up to shore in low tide as did so many others.

Though the injury gave him a deep, four-inch horizontal gash and a concussion, it wouldn't have been fatal to him by itself on dry land. Falling where he did, he was drowning during his unconsciousness. Then his lizard brain in his changeling mind kicked in subconsciously and morphed him into an octopus. Four days later he morphed again, this time into a ghost crab, otherwise known as a sand crab, before he finally regained consciousness. Then he walked himself to shore to look around.

He could see that the invasion had been successful, if for no other reason than the graves registration teams in the Quartermaster Corps had nearly finished recovering the bodies of the fallen Allied soldiers. He walked up the beach past the Gela bluffs and lay down about six feet inside the tree line and fell into a deep sleep.

The next day after the beach was completely vacant, he morphed back into his Corporal John A. Rabbit self, complete in his uniform, web gear, and rifle. He used his cotton bandage to wrap around his head. What he didn't have, was an antiseptic salve to counteract infection, but from what he could feel, his cut was healing without much infection. Perhaps it was due to the salt water. Still, it hurt like the dickens.

Staring up at the sky flat on his back, he realized he had two options. Seek out his fellow 1st Infantry Division compadres or perhaps seek out a party of Italian partisans who were fighting in concert with the Allies against the Italian Fascist soldiers and the German Nazi occupiers.

Hmmm. What were the pros and cons of each?

He knew how to soldier in a conventional Army unit.

Assuming they didn't decide to ship him back stateside due to his injuries, he could pick up with what was left of Able Company and soldier on with them. That would be the easier, more familiar route.

Joining a band of partisans who used guerrilla warfare against the Axis enemies, living in the woods, hunted by the enemy, living off the land with the support of a sympathetic populace would be more exciting, plus it would still further the American cause. Of course, capture would mean torture and ultimate death - at least as a human or so he presumed.

Jack cogitated on this for a long time. He still felt woozy. Then he chose the latter. He sought a new adventure. He wanted to make a bigger impact than he thought he could as just one of thousands of soldiers. Time would tell.

Chapter 6
The Partisans Find Jack

Jack realized he was famished. He had the contents of one box of C-Rations jammed in the bottom of his pack, but he didn't want to deplete it now since he had no means of replacing it. Therefore, he morphed into a rabbit and grazed to his heart's content on clover and fresh green shoots of grass until he was sated. Yum. Yum. Then he morphed back into his human self. The bad thing about eating clover was that it gave him gas, and he was full of it.

He heard movement coming towards him from deeper within the woods. He hoped this was a party of friendly partisans. Nevertheless, in an abundance of caution, he chambered a round in his rifle which he had yet to fire since the invasion began. He took up a prone fighting position behind a fallen tree and some thick bushes. Then he waited.

Slowly but surely, he could make out at least four individuals spread out about three yards apart, firearms at the ready, creeping his direction. The individual in the center held up his hand and 'popped a squat'. The others stopped and squatted, too. Then the leader spoke loudly, "Lo sappiano tu sei lì. Fatti vedere o spareremo noi."

Being a changeling, Jack understood what was said. It was, "We know you are there. Show yourself or we'll shoot." Jack didn't want them to know he understood Italian, so he replied in English, "I'm an American soldier. Are you friend or foe?"

"Amici degli Americani."

Even a non-Italian speaker understood that amici meant friend as in amigo, so Jack stood, but he was still prepared to fight if necessary.

Five individuals stood. One was a woman dressed in men's clothing. They lowered their weapons and began approaching in his direction, still arrayed in a properly spaced offensive line. Jack met them halfway. Then the leader spoke in English. He asked, "Why are you here? Why are you not with the other Americans?"

Jack replied, "How do you know English so well?"

"In my previous life I was a secondary school English teacher. Why are you here?"

"I was wounded in the landing. I just regained consciousness. What day is it?"

"That was six days ago. Today is July 16th. Come with us and we will get you some medical treatment. You don't look so good."

"Do you fight the Germans?"

"Of course, and the Italian Fascists."

"Me too. Glad to meet you all. Show me the way. I will follow."

One man, serving as a scout, turned to lead the way back deeper into the woods. Jack followed him and the others followed Jack. He noticed that they were all armed, carrying a mix of long guns. Two carried the German Army's standard issue rifle, the bolt-action Karabiner 48k, which shot the 7.92 millimeter cartridge; the leader had the German Army's new semi-automatic rifle, the Gewehr 43 which fired the same cartridge; one was equipped with a match grade double barrel Benelli 12-gauge shotgun; and the woman carried an Italian Army bolt-action Carcano Modello 91 rifle which shot the 6.5 millimeter cartridge. Two had a German 'potato masher' hand grenade tucked into their belts. They were all wearing dark civilian garb, including the woman who was also wearing baggy trousers. She was young and had a nice face, even enchanting. She wore a blue bandanna on her head covering her dark brown hair.

They walked quickly, but quietly. The way was heavily forested, rugged, and all uphill. Close to an hour later, they emerged into a clearing with a small bucolic village. Call it rustic. Jack wondered what its name was. He doubted that it would show up on any map, except maybe for a 1:10,000 topographical map. The population was probably less than a hundred. It had perhaps a dozen houses and three or four small businesses. He didn't see any electric lines, meaning no telephones. He did see a variety of horses, mules, donkeys, wagons, and two-wheeled carts, but no motorcars, likely because there were no roads. Only trails and footpaths. It was as though he had stepped back into the late 19th century. Nobody spoke, but several of the villagers nodded or smiled as they passed by. They went to the humble abode of one Dottore E. Rossi and knocked.

The good doctor answered at once and they all stepped inside. He took Jack into his office to check his injuries. The leader followed. The doctor examined Jack carefully. Then he spoke in broken English, "Your wound is healing nicely by itself." Then he pulled a small tube of salve out of a drawer and handed it to Jack, saying, "Apply this three times a day until you run out or the wound is heeled." Jack started to hand him an American two-dollar bill in remuneration, but he shook his head vigorously and exclaimed, "If I get caught with this, they will shoot me! Go with God in peace." Jack thanked him, and then the partisans and he left.

They walked north out of the village to a tidy goat farm where they approached the barn. A 30-ish woman, quite attractive, was hanging wet garments on a clothesline up close to the house. She looked at them noncommittally but didn't speak and they didn't either.

They walked past her and entered the barn. Jack saw that there was one small table and chair situated in the middle of the floor. It was occupied by a thin bald man wearing round, wire-rimmed glasses. He looked to be about 40 years of age. He was dressed like all the others, yet Jack felt himself in the presence of great intellect. He thought the man comported himself more like a college professor or a scientist than a goatherd. He seemed peaceful enough, but a 9-millimeter Beretta Model 1934 pistol was laying on the table next to his right hand. It was obvious he was prepared for danger.

He was studying a map and taking notes when they entered. The leader motioned for them to take a seat on any of the half dozen bales of hay, arranged in such a way that it was apparent they were placed as seating for visitors while meeting with this man of eminence. They sat, and then the leader of the partisans approached the highly esteemed man.

The leader spoke, showing a great degree of deference. He pointed to Jack and speaking in Italian said, "We found this American soldier near the battle site at Gela. He was wounded. Dottore Rossi examined his injury and gave him some medicine. What would you have us to do with him, Capitano?"

The capitano studied Jack carefully, and then asked him in English, "What is your first name, Corporal? We don't use surnames here. Why are you not with your unit?"

"Captain, my name is Jack. I'm a member of the U.S. 1st

Infantry Division. I understand it's been six days since I was rendered unconscious by a bullet while wading to shore in chest-deep water. Truthfully, I can't believe I survived.

"Although I have no reason not to return to my unit, I think I could be of more use here fighting with Allied partisans against the Nazis and Fascists - at least for the time being. I'm a sniper, although my current assignment is as an assistant squad leader in a rifle company. My civilian occupation was as a distiller of illegal corn liquor, although I was never caught."

"I see. Are you a deserter, Jack? Would the American Army shoot you if you returned?"

"No. Of course not. I've received two citations for bravery, and were I to return today, they would award me a second Purple Heart for wounds sustained in combat - my first being in the Great War in France, and the second for my wound here at the Battle of Gela."

"Jack, you do know that if you were ever captured fighting as a partisan, you would be shot or hung without fail. At least if you were captured fighting with your division, you would most likely be interned in a POW camp."

"I do. I'm not saying that I would never want to return to the 1st Division. I do. It's just that I would prefer to fight here for at least a little while with your men. I think I would be an asset. What say you?"

"We call ourselves 'Il Patrioti Invisibil.' Do you know what that means?"

"The Invisible Patriots."

"Exactly. I would like to think we are apolitical, but unfortunately that is not possible. Our current government has betrayed all the people. We who are gathered here are neither communists, nor socialists, nor anarchists. We seek a peaceful life with limited government interference such as you have in America - a democratic nation of capitalists. Nevertheless, we hide in the wilderness from the oppressors and use our meager resources in furtherance of our cause, which is to free Italy from the usurpers. We are labeled as outlaws and would be killed without mercy if they ever found us.

"Can you understand our internal anguish? We use violent methods in furtherance of peace. It sounds so contradictory, but it's the nature of Mankind. Conquer or be conquered so that is what we do. Each of us uses a nom de guerre in an effort to conceal our identities, and sometimes to strike fear in the hearts of our enemies. Mine is Alante, or Atlas to you Americans. I am the regional capitano. What would you call yourself?"

"Il Fantasma."

"Ah, The Ghost, so you do speak Italian."

"Yes, to some degree. Don't ask me to write an essay."

"Of course not. I suspect that you are a man of many hidden talents, Jack. We will try you out on a probationary period in La Squadra dei Lupo, since it was Il Lupo who brought you to me. You will obey him without question. Il Lupo is your Sergente. If you don't work out, we will return you to the American Army posthaste. Understood?"

"Understood."

"That will be all. Il Lupo, take Il Fantasma to your lair. Find him some suitable clothes. Allow him to store whatever belongings he won't need for your missions so he will have them when he returns to the Americans. Instruct him on the way we do things. Make sure he doesn't carry anything on him which would compromise his identity. Clear?"

"Sì, Capitano."

"Once you've done that, come back to see me. I will give you orders for your next mission."

"Sì."

They departed, walking another mile or so, on yet another rocky and uphill path, until they came to an old cabin and outbuilding which appeared to have been abandoned years ago. It had a veranda across the front. He saw windows on either side of the door, and one on the side facing the shed. The circular tin chimney which was three feet above the roof line (to prevent sparks from landing on the wooden shingle hip roof and catching on fire), was emitting a tiny bit of smoke.

Jack noticed at least two cords of firewood stacked up next to the exterior right wall. He also noticed the door did not have a lock. They stepped inside. He saw that the door could be locked from the inside by a stout wooden brace, and that the windows had internal heavy wooden shutters.

This was a one-room cabin. It had six single cots on the right side of the room lined up like an Army barracks. Personal items were stored in short wooden boxes under the beds. The bed at the end farthest away from the door had a curtain made from a sheet around it. The one next to it was empty and Il Lupo assigned it to Jack.

The furniture included an old round oak table with six wooden chairs pushed in around it. It had a pot belly stove at the rear, which had a flat surface on the top used to heat food. On the right of the stove was a wooden box containing more firewood.

The other side of the rear wall had a wooden counter with a white porcelain sink and a faucet with a hand pump. There was shelving along the left side of the wall filled with pots and pans, dishes, canned and boxed food, a variety of boxes with ammunition, towels, blankets, and other sundry items. There were pegs on the walls all around the room, some in use with clothes and blankets hanging on them.

Il Lupo said, "This is our living quarters. We share the cleaning, cooking, woodcutting, washing, and other chores. Each person shares equally. The privy is 15 meters behind the cabin. Make sure you are always armed when you go. We try to observe each person's privacy to the limited extent that we can. La squadra now has six members, including you. Here we call each other by his first name, but nowhere else. I will make the introductions. We sleep in order of rank except for Vittoria since she is a woman. She sleeps at the end.

"My name is Enrico. My moniker, as you know, is Il Lupo, meaning the wolf.

"Second in command is Alfonso, whose moniker is Psico, meaning psycho because he is half crazy. He's also our explosives expert. Did I not say he was half crazy?

"Benito is third. His moniker is Goblin, same as in English, because he is a wizard at playing nasty tricks on il nemico, otherwise known as the enemy to English speakers.

"Carlo is fourth. His moniker is La Scimmia, or the monkey, since he is our best tree climber and lookout. He is also our fastest runner.

"Vittoria is fifth. Her moniker is La Lama, or the blade, because she uses one deftly to kill our enemies so beware and treat her with the utmost respect. She is like our sister. She is also our team medic.

"And you, Jack, are sixth, and your moniker, like we all know, is Il Fantasma. You are the very last in rank and will obey the orders of everyone above you, just like we all do. One day soon I hope we will see how good of a sniper you actually are. We only have one pair of binoculars, so your tasking, properly done, will require great skill without a scope since we can all see you don't have one. I hope you are as good as you say you are. If so, you will be a tremendous asset.

"Everyone, introduce yourself to Jack and make him feel welcome like a brother.

"Jack, before introductions begin, you should know since the loss of Alfredo, we have been short one freedom fighter, and it has made our work much more difficult. Sadly, he fell to his death along a bluff, running from a small patrol of Germans who were on a scouting mission to find us. Alfredo was using his head when he fled, because his flight path took them away from our lair. That was three months ago, and he has been greatly missed by us all since then. He could play the violin like a songbird."

They all smiled at Jack, shook his hand, and greeted him warmly. Jack actually felt welcomed by them as a group for the first time all day. He thought it odd that American soldiers usually treated new guys like they were lepers. It made no sense to him.

"Jack, Vittoria will find you something else to wear to help you blend in. Vittoria, don't overlook an appropriate hat. Jack, for most of our missions, all you will need is your rifle, ammo, knife, water, and maybe some food. Take a compass if you have one. Don't take more than you actually need on any mission. We travel light. We are seldom out for more than 24 hours.

"By the way, how much ammo do you have? I ask because the only way we can get ammunition for a Garand would be if we got it from a dead American soldier. If we come across any, that is what we will do, but it's unlikely we will anytime in the near future."

"Enrico, my cartridge belt is full with ten 8-round clips. In addition, I have ten additional clips in my pack. We came well prepared for the invasion of Gela."

"That should be enough for several months. We do everything we can to avoid engaging in an extended shootout. Typically, we kill an enemy or two and fade back into the woods. We also pick up our brass if we can to make it more difficult for them to identify our weaponry. We do all we can to save ammo, which we always have to scrounge.

"Our number one mission is to live so we can fight another day. If we killed 20 but lost two, we would be in a dire predicament. Understand?"

"I do. Nobody wants a friend to get wounded or killed."

"That's right. Just so you know, Il Patrioti Invisibil is a compartmentalized fighting entity. We are not an army. We have been fighting Il Fascisti and the Nazis since 1939. I have no idea how many strong we are altogether, but I believe us to be more than a hundred, divided into squads similar to ours. I know very few patriots outside of our cell.

"I report to Alante. He assigns our missions. I do the planning and supervise the execution. If I pull a trigger, it usually means something went seriously wrong, like walking into an ambush. At that point, one of us will most likely need to extract us through the use of one of the few German hand grenades that we have acquired. Normally, the Germans only issue them to soldiers going into battle. The rear echelon troops usually don't have them."

"That's good to know. I have five American hand grenades

we can utilize to that same effect. In all my battles, so far, I have only needed to use a grenade once."

"Jack, you are either lucky or really good. Either way, that's good for us.

"Carlo, what do we eat for supper tonight?"

"I caught three hares in my snares. I've been cooking beans all day. We will also have some biscotto. Plus, I purchased a gallon of vino from Signora Gallo, which I paid for from our stash of German marks. She only charged me one."

"Carlo, you are such a great provider. Bravo.

"Benito, after Jack gets some suitable garments, take him out. Familiarize him with our surroundings, including sentry sites, and early warning devices.

"Alfonso, take Jack with you tonight for the first watch.

"Vittoria, you have the second.

"Jack, you will be on second watch tomorrow.

"I'm going to see the captain to get our next mission. I'll be back in time for supper. Ciao."

Vittoria took her assignment seriously and searched through two steamer trunks looking for the right clothes for Jack. She came up with a pair of blue, loose fitting dungarees, a brown leather belt six inches too long, a long sleeve, blue cotton work shirt with a frayed collar, a brown, hip-length, canvas farmer's jacket, a blue bandanna, and a grey felt fedora, which fit like it was made just for him. She also found some brogans, which fit nearly as well as his combat boots, but were much lighter. He couldn't decide if he liked them better or not.

She also found two empty storage boxes for him to stash his belongings under his cot, not least of which was his wallet, dog tags, wristwatch, and anything else which might give away his

American identity. Jack decided that for standard missions, besides his rifle and two extra clips of ammo, the only other Army gear he would take was the bayonet and his compass. It went without saying that he always carried a small pocket notebook and a lead pencil in his shirt pocket. He also decided to put one of his five grenades in his coat pocket for emergency use only.

Vittoria was a great scrounger because while Jack was futzing around deciding what to carry and what to leave under his cot, she found him an old Italian Army canteen with a cork stopper and a leather shoulder strap nobody had laid claim to, plus a working man's one-dollar pocket watch on a leather thong. It seemed to keep time fairly well, as in only losing three minutes a day, in comparison with the others' watches. Jack was very thankful for everything she came up with.

When he was ready, Benito took him all around the lair about a half mile in each direction. He pointed out landmarks and safe hiding places. But first, he introduced Jack to the two mare mules stabled in the shed, named Gemma and Grazia, which they rode or packed whenever they needed to get someplace in a hurry or pick up supplies. Today, they saddled up and inside of an hour, Jack understood the geography surrounding the lair, perhaps as far as a mile in diameter. It was rugged terrain. Riding sure beat walking.

Benito's English was broken, so for the most part they conversed in Italian. Jack asked the name of the village they had stopped in. He said it was called Speranza - Hope in English - and said he grew up there. His family still lives there. His papa is both a goatherd and a cobbler. His brother is a blacksmith, and his sister is married to a furniture maker. Assuming he survived the war, Benito planned to move back there and marry his sweetheart, whose name is Camilla. He planned to follow in his father's footsteps.

By the time they returned, groomed, and fed the mules, Enrico had come back, and Carlo had supper ready. They sat in their usual places. Enrico said a brief prayer. Then they gobbled up all the food. Not a morsel remained. Nobody spoke while they ate, but all were anxiously awaiting news from Enrico regarding their next mission.

After the meal and a long pregnant pause, Enrico finally gave them the briefing they had all been waiting for. He said, "Listen up. We have a new mission, and it's quite dangerous.

"We will begin tomorrow with a surveillance of the Nazi outpost near the village of Fattoria, 10 kilometers (about 6 miles) north of here, taking as many days as we need to set up so we can get away clean. Jack will be our 'the tip of the spear'.

"We're going to eliminate the Nazi general who is in charge of the territorial Waffen-SS. (Armed Schutzstaffel - the black uniformed, combat branch of the Nazi Party, who wore a skull insignia on their uniforms, and served under the overall command of Heinrich Himmler, who was responsible for the death of thousands of Jews, noncombatants, the physically and mentally handicapped, non-Aryans, homosexuals, and various other 'ethnic undesirables'.)

"The target is Brigadefuhrer Franz Hoffman, a generale di brigada to us, or a brigadier general to you, Jack. He will be here one day only on Wednesday, July 28th, in the afternoon to inspire his troops. Our goal is to snipe him from as great a distance as we can, undetected to facilitate our escape and to make it impossible for them to point the finger at any specific partisan group. This is in an effort to prevent wholesale reprisals against the local citizenry. Personally, I believe that is wishful thinking, but we'll all hope for the best.

"This man is a monster and an architect of many horrendous atrocities. This is a sanctioned assassination, coming down from the very top leadership of Il Patrioti Invisibil. We have never undertaken anything this audacious before. Is everyone fully committed to do this? Our lives will all be in extreme peril."

Enrico looked deep into the eyes of each member of the squad, including Jack. Nobody blinked. Four voices in unison, Jack being a split second behind the rest because he didn't know this custom, replied "aye".

"The ayes have it.

"Jack, what is the farthest distance that you can be assured of making a fatal shot?"

"My longest ever is 450 yards. However, light, wind, rain, elevation, and movement, all factor in."

"That's roughly 400 meters. Everyone keep that in mind while you're scouting. We'd prefer something less than that, but we must have cover and concealment and most importantly, we have to have a safe escape route.

"We've all seen the pomp and circumstance, not to mention the precision the Germans put into everything they do. I'm waiting for more intelligence from Alante, but we think Hoffman will address the troops from one of the platforms they have in the assembly area for the physical fitness instructors in particular, but others as well. They may even construct a special platform. Either way, that would make for a clear, nearly stationary shot assuming he isn't too encumbered with slobbering lackeys.

"Don't get too fixated on this idea. This is Plan A. We will also need a viable Plan B. We probably won't get another opportunity for a high-level target like Hoffman ever again, so we must get both options right.

"Anyone have family or friends in Fattoria?"

There were no takers.

"That's what Alante thought. It's just as well. What that means is none of us can just show up there without having a good reason and we don't have one. If it becomes imperative and Alante doesn't have someone to feed us the intel we need, we'll have to come up with a reason. However, our goal is not to be seen by anyone in Fattoria, so we won't have the Nazis or the Fascists tracking us back to here.

Tomorrow, everyone except for Carlo and I will scout the area. Alfonso and Benito will be one team and Vittorio and Jack will be the other. Alfonso, your team can take the mules. Vittorio, you take the binoculars. Take something to eat with you. I want you to watch until it gets dark. We'll have a late supper. I'm making spaghetti and meatballs.

"You all know what you need to do. Oh! I nearly forgot. I have two hand-drawn maps - one for each team. Any questions?

"None? Okay. Cleanup first, and first night watch take your post."

Chapter 7
A Pleasant Non-Military Surprise

On Saturday, July 17th, they were all up with the chickens in a manner of speaking, since they didn't have any chickens living at the lair. The foxes had gotten them all, and they had been too busy to replace them. However, Enrico promised they would very soon. Dawn was just breaking, so Carlo lit one of the oil lamps. Jack brushed his teeth out on the verandah and rinsed his mouth from his new, old Italian canteen with the leather shoulder strap. Then he collected the items he would take with him, putting the smaller things in a canvas shoulder bag. It wasn't much.

They each drank a three-ounce cup of that supercharged espresso tar the Italians call coffee and ate some deer jerky and several plums from the nearly full bushel near the sink. Jack realized he must adapt to their culture if he wanted to get along, but he did miss eating sausage and grits for breakfast and drinking American coffee.

Vittoria grabbed a small loaf of Italian bread, a chunk of goat cheese, and more plums for their lunch. Then they headed for the woods. Jack had a compass, but he didn't really know where he was, so he was thankful Vittoria knew the way. He could tell they were headed northwest, but that was all. He did the best he could to memorize some landmarks, because the trail was indistinct. At least they weren't going uphill, and in fact, may have been dropping slightly in elevation. Along the way, Jack saw plenty of deer scat. He would try to bag a doe when it became his time to cook. It took them two hours of steady walking to arrive.

The tree line stopped abruptly at the edge of a grassy field about 50 feet in depth, which ran laterally along the front of the woods for at least 200 yards. Straight ahead, the field extended to a series of rocky knolls, maybe ten feet tall, all of which were covered with scrubby bushes. They crawled up one in the center and took in the view.

A two-lane dirt road was 30 feet beneath them and ran generally in a north-south direction on the east side of the small town of Fattoria. The Nazi compound was south of the town about a quarter mile. It was large enough to house at least a company of infantry, assuming it was manned to capacity. It was cordoned off with farm fencing, featuring coiled barbed wire along the top. The main gate was centered on the south side. A smaller gate was situated on the east side, almost directly across from where they were perched. It didn't appear to be in use today.

The compound was busier than a beehive being robbed by a bear with a sweet tooth. New bleachers were going up, being constructed by what appeared to be a cadre of conscripted Italians. They were not wearing uniforms or POW garb, so it was hard to tell. Nevertheless, two guards armed with MP40, Schmeisser 9-millimeter submachine guns were posted to watch while they worked.

Jack took some notes and estimated distances. Assuming the speech platform was centered facing the bleachers, the shot would be about 300 yards - three football fields, measuring distances like they taught him in the Army. He could make that shot easily from where he was. He had plenty of concealment and an easy escape route out of view from the camp. The camp did have one guard tower, but it was on the other side of the camp, situated where the focus of attention was the front gate. Depending upon where they parked Hoffman's automobile, Jack might have an unobstructed shot at him upon either his arrival or departure as a Plan B.

Jack had seen all he really needed to see until the speech platform was erected. The only other need to know information was the route Hoffman's command vehicle would use to come and go. He could see two possibilities and the area where they parked command vehicles. He assumed Hoffman would be driven up next to the main entrance to the building, but maybe not. They could have another entrance on the west side of the building that he couldn't see from here. He hoped Alfonso and Benito checked out that side of the compound.

Enrico's instructions were specific about watching until it got dark, so Jack decided to make the most of his time. Vittoria was an attractive woman who dumbed down her looks by the clothes she wore as a partisan.

You know how much time Jack had spent around women? Nearly none, and he was starved for it. He had never had a girlfriend. He didn't remember his mother very well. It had been too long and his memory of her had faded. He hadn't spent much time around his sister, Phoebe. He didn't know what to say to women, especially one as attractive as Vittoria, but he decided to give it a go anyway.

"Nice day, huh?"

"Yes."

"How did you know the way here?"

"I grew up close by, near Gela, in fact. I've never been anywhere else, yet I'm 23 years old. The Germans killed my family three years ago when I was away helping tend to a sick friend. When I returned, I saw my papa and mama and both of my brothers bound, tortured and no longer among the living, I gathered a few of my things as quickly as I could and fled to Grandmama's. She hid me until I could get to Hope to enlist in the Resistance. Dottore Rossi and his wife helped me recover from my grief and to channel my anger.

"This is my life now. I've forgotten what it was like to be carefree, to go to an ice cream parlor, to celebrate the holidays with my family, or even how to fall in love."

"Goodness! Why did they kill your family?"

"Because a Fascist neighbor reported my father for passing messages to the Resistance. That much I know for sure. I'm pretty sure that after they tied everyone up in the kitchen chairs, they tortured everyone to make Papa talk. He probably did to save the family, but when they extracted everything he knew, they shot each of them between the eyes. It was the SS, just like these animals here in this compound. You cannot imagine the depth of my hatred for them. If I could, I would kill them all!

"You know why they call me La Lama? Because I went to the informer's house late one night and slit her throat ear to ear. I even left a note saying, 'La Lama sees and knows all.' She was my first, but not the last.

"So . . . now that you know I'm damaged goods, you may not want to work with me. Now men are scared to entertain romantic notions about me, afraid I might go off my rocker and slit their throats in their sleep."

"This is war, Vittoria, and like it or not, the rules are different in war. I, for one, already have romantic notions about you, but alas, I'm twice your age and besides that, I know from what

Enrico said, it is forbidden."

"Jack, that's the sweetest thing a man ever said to me! You think I'm pretty dressed like a transient bum?"

"I do. I have never had a sweetheart. I don't know how to talk to women but somehow, I can talk to you. I know without ever seeing underneath your garments you are a beautiful woman. The beauty within you cannot be contained by garments of any sort. It sorrows me that I will never taste of your pleasures."

"How do you know? How can you be so sure? I might not be able to contain my passion."

"I know, because once I became your lover, I could never keep my eyes or my hands off of you. Everyone could see it in my behavior and hopefully yours too. Enrico would send me back to my unit or the next best thing to it. Your reputation would be sullied.

"Besides, we both know the time will come when I must return to the U.S. Army. I can't take you with me or I would. That day will break my heart. Even so, after the war is over if we both survive and you still feel this way about me, I would move mountains to bring you to America if you were interested, but perhaps you would not like it there.

"I live in the mountains of Eastern Kentucky in a cabin similar to the lair. For the past 20 years I made my living by distilling and selling illegal corn liquor spirits. I have a little money set aside but it's not a lot. I never really needed a lot. Then there's the age issue. Would you sign on to a marriage where you will likely outlive me by 20 years?"

"Jack, no man has even spoken to me like you speak. I've known you for one day only and you've seared yourself into my heart forever. I have a proposition for you. I will wait for you after you return to the American Army if you will wait for me. If you still love me and I still love you and you send for me, I will come to America. What more can I say? Is it a deal? Should we shake hands or seal it with a kiss?"

"Deal, but how would I ever find you?"

"I have the same question for you."

"I have an address, John A. Rabbit, c/o Gerard S. Twyman, Rabbit Hollow, Lawrence County, Kentucky, U.S.A. I will write it down right now and give it to you to keep. Gerard is my cousin. His farm is adjacent to mine. Mail it to him just in case I haven't gotten home yet. What about you?"

"Easy. Vittoria Maria Bianchi, c/o Dottore E. Rossi, #12, Speranza, Italy. How could you ever forget that? You've already been there."

"I couldn't forget under normal circumstances, but I will jot down a cryptic note in case I do. You see, I had amnesia for a long time after my injuries in the Great War. I didn't even know my name. (He wrote in his pocket notebook.) Okay. Done. What would you like to do now?"

"What I'd really like to do, you won't do with me."

"Believe me when I say that it's all I can do not to, but I'm refraining to protect you. Please don't tempt me anymore right now. My willpower is limited."

"You are a chivalrous soul, Corporal John A. Rabbit. I will have sweet dreams about you tonight. Tell me all about Lawrence County, Kentucky. I bet it's not even on a map."

"It's not, unless you have a Kentucky state roadmap and I'm not even certain of that because I never checked, but I can tell you . . . "

The hours passed too quickly, but dusk finally came, and they began their journey back. This time it was more difficult because it was hard to see in the forest, but Vittoria found the way. Everyone was waiting.

Enrico's spaghetti was marvelous, and he made a double portion. Even so, there were no leftovers. Alfonso and Benito, riding mules, had canvassed the entire area around Fattoria. They'd added notations on their handwritten map, which Vittorio added to the one she had. They said the safest place to set up would be on one of the knolls on the east side of the compound.

Jack confirmed that. He said he could make the shot with just one of the others for cover and to lead him back to the lair expeditiously. He also suggested they ride the mules. They could tether them inside the tree line for a quicker getaway.

Enrico replied, "Jack, it sounds good, and you sound confident. It's hard for me to believe it will be so easy. Nothing's ever that easy. You and I will ride over there tomorrow so you can show me. Also, what about Plan B?"

"Plan B is to take him when he goes back to his motorcar to depart, assuming he's parked up near the front entrance to the building where the commandant parks."

"Very good. Beginning tomorrow, we will only deploy one two-man team to watch from the site Jack has selected. Except for Carlo, the rest of you have tomorrow off. Carlo, stock up on provisions to include stocking the cave in the event we can't stay here. The Nazis will go berserk and scorch the earth looking for us even though they will have no idea who we are. Any questions?"

No one spoke.

After cleaning up, Jack and the entire squad took their chairs out to the veranda. All the men except for Jack smoked their pipes. Jack smoked a cigar. Carlo produced another jug of Senora Gallo's delicious 'Dago Red' wine. It was the perfect way to cap off the day.

Sunday morning, after a breakfast of espresso, a ham sandwich, and more plums, Enrico and Jack departed on horseback. They cut yesterday's time in transit by more than half. The compound was not so busy in that this was the Sabbath, but Enrico could see where the speech platform was being erected and that the trip to and from the woods was concealed from view by the enemy. The camp commander, Major Reinhard Weber, stepped out of the building with several subordinates. He was examining the progress of the construction and from his body language and strong gesticulations, he wasn't very pleased with it.

Jack said, "How would you like to have him for your boss?"

Enrico replied, "It would be impossible. At some point I would have to kill him. Running away would not be sufficient."

"What if I did it for you right after I take out Hoffman?"

"Think you would have enough time?"

"Yes, assuming they stood close to each other."

"Hmmm. I would like that. It would throw the rest of the Nazis here at this post in a tizzy with their leadership killed before their very eyes. The Germans don't transition very well when their leaders are deposed or removed. They've spent too many years in absolute subordination licking the master's boots. This could really help our fight against the Hun.

"I'll run it by Alante. I think he will go for it if for no other reason than once we use this site, we will never be able to use it again. They'll knock down the knolls or post guards up here.

Killing Major Weber at a later date would be much more difficult than if we turned this into a two-fer.

"Come on. I've seen enough. I'll go see Alante and get his take."

The rest of the day was spent in recreational pursuits. Jack and Vittoria played chess.

When Jack learned that he was expected to make supper on Monday evening he took Vittoria with him to scout for a deer. He found a nice doe and he took her down with a head shot about 100 yards away - no wasted meat. He gutted and field dressed it while Vittoria went back to get the mules.

Upon their return, he hung it upside down and began the butchering. The others were excited to have fresh meat so Alfonso conferred with Jack, and they decided that Alfonso's plan to fix bacon and eggs would be postponed until breakfast. They now had enough deer meat to last at least two days and maybe three. Vittoria and Benito went to Hope to purchase bread, butter, milk, fresh vegetables, strawberries, vino, and even some pastries for a treat. Everyone felt like celebrating, especially Vittoria since she now had a secret sweetheart.

That night they ate like royalty. Everyone was jolly. After cleaning up and washing the dishes, they all retired to the verandah for wine and smokes.

When all were mellow Enrico said, "Jack suggested he eliminate Major Weber right after he takes out General Hoffman. Alante gave us the go ahead. With that in mind, Alante says the Nazis are bound to murder at least a dozen or so innocent civilians for reprisals, probably from Fattoria, but maybe other places as well. Of course, they will do all they can to identify the assassins but if we do this right they probably won't look for us.

For one thing, besides Alante and us, no one knows we have a sniper in our ranks.

"I'm assigning Alfonso to be Jack's guide, and backup should they run into trouble. They will take the mules. Alfonso, take an alternate route once it's done and do what you can to avoid leaving a trail. Go directly to the cave until we see how the Nazis respond.

"Carlo, I want you somewhere high up in a tree in the woods where you can see the Nazi compound. I want you to watch for which direction they go searching for the assassins. For crying out loud, stay concealed so they don't spot you! Once you know, come back here to the lair to fill me in. Benito, you wait at the cave. When Alfonso and Jack return, you bring the mules and come back here.

"Alante will have some of our brothers and sisters out and about collecting intelligence, which he will pass to me.

"Vittoria will stay back with me to carry out any unforeseen missions. As soon as I get a read on which ways the Nazis are searching, I will decide if it's safe to stay here or if we all need to stay in the cave. Nobody but us knows it even exists and it's difficult to find, so it's the safest place to stand down that I can think of. Of course, we would all be more comfortable here.

"Tomorrow, Carlo and Benito will watch the compound. We still have ten days until the mission. Get some rest."

They finished up and padded off to bed one by one. Most of their prep work was done.

Chapter 8
The Day Has Finally Come

On Wednesday, July 28th, 1943, they were awakened at 2 o'clock by Enrico's old windup alarm clock, assuming any of them had really been able to sleep. They all knew today would alter their lives for a very long time. They had never killed an enemy of this importance before. All of their previous targets had been informers, Axis sympathizers, or low-ranking enemy soldiers. That in itself stirred up a big enough hornets' nest.

On this morning, Jack wore his web belt with ten clips of cartridges just in case he didn't return to the lair for a while. He also took three boxes of cigars.

Alfonso led them along a circuitous route in the event that the Nazis managed to come up with a good tracker. Probably not, but it didn't hurt to take extra precautions. They had plenty of time. He and Jack were on site by 4:30. Now it was time to wait. This gave Jack plenty of time to think about Vittoria. He'd never felt passions like this in his centuries-long, changeling life. Were he alone, he would have transformed himself into a rabbit and grazed on the luscious green grass behind him. Ah, well. Maybe there was a way after all.

Before dawn broke, he told Alfonso he had to relieve himself. He walked back to the tree line away from the mules and changed into a rabbit. He left rabbit droppings instead of human waste. Nobody would be the wiser. Then he crept up just past the trees and grazed on some fresh green grass. When he was sated, he morphed back into Jack the human.

Upon his return, Alfonso said, "You took so long that I was afraid you'd gotten lost."

"No. Sorry. The call of Mother Nature was urgent. Anything happening?"

"No, but more lights are on in the building."

A little after noon, the big black Mercedes Benz bearing twin Nazi flags carrying General Hoffman passed by, coming from the north. It was preceded by two soldiers riding motorcycles. They were waived through the south entrance of the compound by low-ranking guards eager to please. Just prior to the arrival, Major Weber ordered all troops not otherwise occupied to assemble in the bleachers and stand at attention as soon as the general arrived. Once he went into the building they could all stand down.

Weber met Hoffman outside the front door of the building. He saluted crisply and got down on his hands and knees and licked Hoffman's boots. (That might be a little hyperbolic, but you get the drift. Imagine brown-nosing at its highest level.) Then they went inside and out of sight.

Alfonso said, "You see that? This could be a problem. If the Nazis realize the shots came from one of these knolls, those motorcycles could be on us before we could get to the mules."

Jack replied, "If they get their wits about them too quickly, we'll have to take them out too. Personally, I think they'll be more focused on their fallen demigod. Believe me, what we're about to do is so unanticipated they'll be witless plenty long enough for us to slip away."

Alfonso replied, "What if we took out the bikes by shooting a hole in their gas tanks after you get Hoffman and Weber? As much as I'd like to waste a Nazi thug, if we shoot the riders someone else could still ride the bikes in an emergency such as this."

"Righto. Keep an eye on both of the motormen and if they act like they're going to come in pursuit that's what we'll do. Do you think you could hit the gas tanks from here?"

"Doubtful. My gift is in ripping the testicles of Nazis and Fascists out of their scrotums with my bare hands. I'd have to be a lot closer than this to be assured of shooting a man, let alone a gas tank on a motorcycle."

"Then I'll do it if it comes to that; however, I think they'll be in a state of shock. For all we know, the bodyguard escorts could be executed on the spot for not saving Hoffman's life."

"Wouldn't that be a nice twist of fate?"

They still had an hour and a quarter to wait for Hoffman to exit the building and ascend the platform to inspire his armed political thugs masquerading as soldiers in their Satanic black uniforms, with a windy speech to remind them all of their racial superiority. Alfonso was getting fidgety, but the Rabbit took it all in stride.

At 1:55, General Hoffman and Major Weber emerged from the building, both standing erect and resplendent in their tailored black uniforms replete with shiny silver skulls and a chest full of medals, looking haughty and invincible. The troops were still assembled, standing at attention in the three rows of newly constructed bleachers.

The two leaders stepped up on the speaker's platform, where they paused long enough to evoke awe and fear and reverence into their troops, or so they thought. They were probably correct, too. The SS was all an-volunteer force, highly vetted to ensure their politics were consistent with the party line. Not a single draftee here on this hallowed ground. No siree!

Hoffman stood on the right, away from Jack. Weber stood to Hoffman's left, but three inches behind in deference to Hoffman's exalted rank. They jammed their right arms high into the sky in the Nazi salute, exclaiming, "Sieg Heil! (meaning hail victory!) The audience followed suit.

That was all Jack needed. His first shot hit Hoffman in the temple on the left side. Before he hit the floor, Weber was dead too, with a fatal shot through his Adams apple which he had exposed to Jack due to his astonished look towards the sound of the shot which slew Hoffman. Weber's blood spewed like a fire hydrant out of control.

It was just like Jack thought it would be. All the survivors were too shocked to react.

Alfonso said, "I recovered your brass. Let's get out of here." They slipped down the knoll, crouched down low, and scampered to the woods. The mules were nervous due to the gunshots, but manageable especially with soothing assurances by their masters.

Once Alfonso and Jack were mounted, they began a slow departure towards the cave, but in a circuitous route. It took more than two hours to arrive. Once again, Jack tried to establish some landmarks but without much success. The best he found was a small creek flowing with cold crystal-clear water where they stopped to let the mules drink, whet their own whistles, and fill their canteens. It turned out to be about a hundred yards from the cave, so it didn't aid much in helping Jack to fix their overall position in his head.

Benito was waiting. He had started a small fire to make some coffee for Alfonso and Jack upon their arrival. He got the coffee brewing the moment he saw them emerge from the woods. He asked, "How did it go? Do you think you were followed? Look, I'm brewing you some coffee. Are you both okay? Everyone's been on pins and needles waiting to hear."

Alfonso replied, "No, we were not followed. All is well. Both targets eliminated. We made a clean getaway. Totally undetected. I can't wait to hear what Carlo saw after the deed was accomplished. Complete chaos from what little I saw before we hoofed it."

"Great news. I'll take the mules back to the lair and tell Enrico. I've stocked the cave with your belongings as well as your cots, bedding, and some grub. Someone will be back before nightfall to fill you in on what we'll do next. Anything else you need me to do?"

Alfonso replied, "No, but be careful. It's anyone's guess what the Nazis will do next. Ditto for Alante. Things will get real dicey now."

Carlo and the mules departed. Jack and Alfonso pulled up a fallen log to sit on. They drank the bitter coffee and indulged in a much-needed smoke.

After a long silence, Alfonso said, "Il Fantasma, you are an incredible marksman. People far and wide will be talking about this for a long, long time. This was a serious blow to our enemy. They will spare no effort looking for Il Fantasma. If you were Alante, what would you do next?"

"I'm no political or military strategist, so I don't know. What I do know is, I wouldn't wait too long before striking again, ideally at another leader to instill fear in their command structure.

"I'm very much afraid the Nazis will murder innocent

civilians in a wholesale manner to keep them at bay, all the while hoping to get a lead on Il Patrioti Invisibil, and me in particular as the shooter. That's assuming they believe Il Patrioti Invisibil was the actual group of freedom fighters who struck this blow, but now that I think about it, I don't see how they could. They pursued Alfredo but never caught him. They apparently gave up looking for us because they haven't come any closer to finding our lair. At any rate, the longer we go without striking again, inflicting fear and more pain on key individuals, the worse it will get for the innocent populace."

"You're probably right, but there are many other partisan groups besides us. I'm sure Alante has coordination with some of them, not to mention the other squads within our own group. Hopefully, some of them will step up and strike a blow for Italy and Democracy. It would draw attention away from us, giving us time to execute another mission even as audacious as this one."

"Agreed."

It seemed like they waited forever to hear back from Enrico. They rooted through the provisions and found some canned beans, bread, a peck of plums, jars of prunes, pickles, and applesauce, goat jerky, coffee, salt, a bushel of red potatoes, a can of lard, a can of condensed milk, a smoked ham wrapped in burlap, three gallons of wine, tins of sardines and tuna fish, a half-gallon of olive oil, a box of brown sugar, and a bushel full of fresh vegetables including peppers, carrots, tomatoes, leaf lettuce, and red cabbage. Jack figured it was enough to last them a week. There was also a three-day old Italian newspaper, matches, candles, and a box of tissues.

They consumed a big meal of ham, pinto beans, a fresh salad

with olive oil, bread, and Dago Red wine. They ate with gusto. As they were cleaning up, Enrico and Vittoria rode in on Gemma and Grazia. It was just before dusk.

After they dismounted and everyone found a makeshift seat, the men lit their smokes, and they all consumed a couple of cups of wine. Finally, Enrico said, "Great job fellows. Just so you know, the Nazis have swarmed Fattoria and murdered 11 innocent citizens, including the mayor in retaliation. We've learned they're bringing in another company of SS to help search for the terrorists who killed their exalted leaders.

"They still don't have the first clue as to whom is responsible, so they plan to swarm the region with the assistance of a second company of stormtroopers, ultimately to intimidate someone into snitching. Call it a seek and destroy mission. This lot is coming from Messina - up in northwest Sicily, Jack - via a dedicated troop train. It will also have their new commander on it, believed to be a Major Fritz Eckhardt, who is supposed to be a rising star in the SS. They're expected to arrive Friday, July 30th, sometime in the afternoon. Being a military train, they do all their own scheduling and as you probably know, compel regular trains to pull onto a siding to allow them to pass."

Jack asked, "How on Earth do you know all this? You must have ears in the telegraph office in Fattoria."

Enrico replied, "What a novel idea! Back to business. Our job is to knock out the train as it traverses the trestle across La Gola del Diavolo (The Devil's Gorge), eight kilometers (five miles) north of Fattoria, making it 16 kilometers (10 miles) from where we are. La Squadra delle Volpe (Fox Squad) will assist us from the north side of the gorge.

"We now have 16 cases of 40-percent dynamite to place on the supports on the south end of the trestle. La Squadra delle Volpe has the same for the north side. We will wire our charges in combination with theirs, but you, Alfonso, will detonate all the charges. If you see you won't have enough dynamite, use it all on the central supports so the train cannot get across. We want it to tumble all the way down, 100 meters (110 yards) to the bottom. We want everyone on that train to perish. No survivors. After the explosion, La Squadra della Volpe will mop up any survivors since their lair is closer to the gorge than ours, while we return here.

"In addition, to enable backup Plan B, both squads are now equipped with two American M-1 bazookas (portable recoilless anti-tank rocket launcher). Each comes with a dozen 60-millimeter recoilless rockets. They claim the range is 370 meters (400 yards), but admit the maximum effective range is only 140 meters (150 yards). These weapons were designed as tank killers, so I don't know how effective they would be on the engine of a train but I'm guessing they would stop it, and that's why we have been provided with two.

"Each bazooka requires a shooter and a loader. This is also why with all your heart, you want the trestle to collapse in the middle so that Plan B, disabling the train with bazookas on the trestle, becomes a moot issue because the follow-up is that we would have to blow up each passenger car with the bazookas before the Nazis could disembark and overwhelm us. That would be do or die with the odds stacked heavily against us.

"One more thing. Bazookas are heavy and cumbersome. They weigh 5.9 kilograms (13 pounds), and they're 137 centimeters long (5 ½ feet), not to mention the size and weight of the rockets. Jack, have you ever fired one before?"

"No. Normally only the heavy weapons platoon has them, but I watched the demonstration in training. They're fairly simple to operate. I'm positive that I could do it. How on Earth did you manage to get the U.S. Army to give these to us?"

"We didn't. My understanding is several crates of bazookas fell off the back of a truck and we just happened to find them."

"Wasn't that providential?"

"God works in mysterious ways.

"We're bugging out 0600 in the morning. You'll have to hump all your own gear because both mules will be loaded down with dynamite, bazookas, recoilless rockets, rope, and other necessary items, so bring whatever you plan to eat while we're gone.

"As I mentioned, I decided to go with you this time. If all goes well, we should be back in the wee hours Saturday morning. Bring lots of ammo - lots - because if we botch this, we'll be pursued by the entire Kraut Army not to mention our own Fascist traitors until eventually, one day, they get us all.

"Any questions? None?"

"Okay. See you all at 0600."

Chapter 9

What is the Opposite of
Building Bridges for Humanity?

For this mission, Jack decided to carry and wear everything he had on his person the day he joined the partisans except for his shot up helmet and liner. It felt great to once again wear his combat boots, which were easier on his feet than the Italian brogans they had given him. He did, however, wear the gray fedora. He had come to love that hat.

Why was he doing this? It was simple. This endeavor had all the earmarks of a mission from which one might never return, and he didn't want to leave anything behind. If he had to flee, he wanted to be as prepared as possible.

Heck! Just consider this. Wiring a train trestle with dynamite is risky enough, especially using an electrical source of detonation. Any errant electrical charge could set it off, which is why Jack preferred using a time fuse you lit with a match or a smoke. The rate of burn on the fuse to the blasting cap is one foot per minute. Measure the distance; cut the fuse to the appropriate length; and wait for it to do its job. Very simple. Very reliable, but slow.

Of course, if there's a long distance from the source of detonation to the charge, which is what this job requires, the traditional method of ignition is impractical without knowing exactly when the train would cross. Demolition is a dangerous business and that's why explosive experts make the big bucks. Stories regarding careless bombers who accidentally blew themselves up are well documented.

Another hazard unmentioned by the strategist of this mission was the possibility of slipping and falling from the trestle stanchions to a most certain death deep in the gorge while setting up the charges. One needed only to miss a single step climbing up or coming down, complicated by the heavy but delicate load one must carry. That is all it would take. Just in case that should happen, remember that it helps to close your eyes during the rapid descent before you bite the dust.

Yet another risk encountered is in setting the charges under the cover of darkness. There's no room for error, and it helps if one can see what he's doing. This task is a little more difficult than scratching your butt at night under the covers, not to mention that the stakes are much greater.

However, on a positive note if they were successful in carrying out this mission, it would eliminate a couple hundred Nazi fanatics in one fell swoop. How many Allied lives would that spare, especially as it relates to the noncombatants? No one knew for sure, but it was bound to be substantial. That is why this was a 'do or die' mission and well worth the risk.

The following morning, they departed on time, but it was rugged going, such that they didn't arrive until almost 1400 hours. Fox Squad was waiting for them on the other side. Enrico and Alfonso met the Fox leaders in the middle of the trestle while the rest of them took a breather. Fortunately, nobody else was anywhere around so far as they could see. Ditto for 'Engine, engine number 9 coming down the railroad line'.

After a half-hour tête-à-tête, Enrico and Alfonse returned. Enrico said, "Listen up. There are eight supports holding up this trestle. We decided to wire just the four in the middle. We're making a redundant firing system, meaning we're double wiring it in the event one set of wire shorts out and doesn't ignite. Also, both sides will be able to detonate although Alfonso will be the primary. Once the entire train is on the track, which will be a total of six passenger cars plus the engine or, so we've been told, then we detonate.

"If Fox sees the train has come nearly halfway across the trestle and we haven't detonated, as in our charge failed to go off, they will detonate. We want the engine with all its weight to pull the rest of the cars with it all the way down to the bottom. Once the engine enters the trestle, it's committed. Even at half speed it won't be able to stop in time to avoid disaster.

"Now comes the hard part. Each stanchion has four sets of X-shaped supports to give it strength. We decided to place charges on the top three. That's four charges on each X, times three X's, times two supports, meaning 24 individual charges for both squads.

"Each squad has 16 boxes of dynamite with 20 sticks per, totaling 320 sticks. Truth is, not a one of us knows how much dynamite this will take to do the job properly, so we decided to make 8-stick bundles which is probably overkill, but we can't risk failure.

"Everyone knows about Murphy's Law. 'Anything that can go wrong, will go wrong.' Do the math. That's 192 sticks per squad being determined not to fail, which means we'll only need to open 10 boxes. Ergo, we'll have plenty left over for another mission or two some other time down the road.

"We will bind the 8-stick charges once we get on the ground down below. After nightfall, the first step will be to bind each bundle to our 24 X's, each with two blasting caps - one for Fox and one for us. The plan is for both squads to do this simultaneously.

"Once both sides have completed that, the next phase will be to string the electrical wiring. Both squads have eight spools of wire, which should be more than enough, even at these distances. Also, each squad will string the other squad's wire after they've strung their own to eliminate the need to cross over to the other squad's supports. We're trying to keep this as simple as possible, so we have no mistakes.

"We can't set the charges until it gets dark. Also, we'll have to climb from the ground up, so we'll assemble down at the bottom while it's still daylight. We'll use two, two-man teams. Alfonse will place the charges on the support nearest our side, and Benito will be his assistant. Jack will set the charges on the other support with Carlo, our monkey climber, to assist. Vittoria will be our lookout topside, and I will handle the mules down under.

"We don't know how long this will take but it wouldn't surprise me if it takes all night. Once we've set the charges, we'll return topside to wait, watch, and rest.

"If any of you think climbing the stanchions with a satchel full of explosives in the dark is daunting, Plan B is even worse. That's why Plan A absolutely has to work.

"Pay very close attention. This is Plan B.

"Each squad will have two bazooka teams deployed and ready to go as soon as we sight the train.

"Understand this. The way I see it, Fox will be sidelined if we go to Plan B unless they can sprout wings and fly because the train will be barreling towards us and away from them. Maybe their real job is to mop up after we are all dead. What else could they do? It's either that or run away. By the time they could get within striking distance to assist, we'd be overrun, and it would be too late to help us.

"Back to Plan B . . . Carlo will be one bazooka shooter, and I will be his loader. Vittoria will be the other shooter, and Benito will be her loader; however, everyone needs to study the bazookas and the rockets so we all can do either job, if necessary.

"The idea is to put as many rockets as we can into the engine to disable it before it gets off the trestle. We know the bazooka was designed to be a tank killer so we hope it will also do the job on a train engine. Nobody knows. Assuming it works and the train is dead in the water, then we put rockets into each of the passenger cars before the stormtroopers can disembark. It would be up to Jack to shoot the ones which do manage to get out.

"During all the chaos, Alfonso will still be busy trying to detonate the charges to save our skins. Now you all understand why Plan B is strictly a last-ditch effort. Just pray that Plan A works as planned.

"If no one has any questions, let's find the best way to get down to the bottom."

They found a well-used path. They halted just before leaving the cover of the forest. Everyone took time to eat and have a smoke. They all took a nap, taking turns on watch. A little before 8, those who were hungry ate again. Then Vittoria took up her surveillance post top-side, and the others prepared to do their specific assignments.

Someone lit a flashlight for just a second across the gorge and Enrico replied in kind. It was time to get to work.

Amongst themselves, they decided to start on the top X and work their way down. Jack began climbing with his rifle slung across his opposite shoulder, and a satchel filled with four bundles of dynamite and a small wooden box of blasting caps. Carlo followed him with eight bundles of dynamite and a hank of rope to bind the bundles to the other X's.

The supports were spaced such that they had footholds all the way up about every eight inches. Jack was thankful they had a waxing moon with a slight breeze and that it wasn't raining. So far, so good. This part didn't take as long as he had thought and an hour later, they were back on the ground.

Next step was stringing Wolf squad's wire. This was a lot more tedious. It required Carlo to climb close-up behind Jack and feed it to him from a spool. This took an hour and a half. The final portion of the job was to string Fox's wire. Because Jack's muscles were screaming bloody murder, never having climbed so much in such a short period of time, his body was getting a little shaky. It took him almost two hours to complete this task.

Alfonso, being Wolf's explosives expert, climbed up after Jack and Carlo came down to inspect Jack's job. He was more than satisfied. Altogether, setting the charges took about five hours. Then they made their way back up to the top of the gorge and found a soft place to sleep in the woods out of sight, but near the train tracks. Everything had gone exceptionally well and thankfully, they had seen nary a passerby or an enemy patrol. All that was left was to hook up the plunger and familiarize themselves with the bazookas.

At daybreak, Enrico got out the binoculars to see if any of the bundles could be spotted. He only saw one, and it was too far away to tell what it was. They were good to go. All they had to do now was wait.

They did have a moment of panic. At 9:27, an unexpected train came barreling down the track going in the opposite direction. After it was gone, Alfonso scrambled down to the gorge to get a closer look at all the bundles. Everything looked intact, so he returned to the top with a sigh of relief plastered across his face.

The timing turned out fortuitously for the partisans because at 1214 hours, they could see the train with a Nazi flag flapping in the breeze coming around the bend on the north side of the gorge. It was going hell for leather. The engineer blew the horn as the train approached the trestle as if to say, "We're coming to empty your lifeblood, you mongrel peasants! Double-dog dare you to try and stop us. We're the master race!" The Day of Reckoning had finally arrived for someone, but whom?

The bazooka teams were poised to go into action but remained inside the tree line. Alfonso hooked the wires to the electric detonator and pulled the plunger up as far as it could go. He said a silent prayer that they had wired everything correctly. Jack took a position on the other side of the tracks, ready to engage any of the enemy who might show his face.

The sound of the approaching train got louder and louder. Jack saw it start across the trestle. He watched as Alfonso tensed just before he slammed the plunger down. He timed it perfectly and the entire midsection of the track blew up, showering the air with fire, smoke, steel, wood, and other debris. The explosion was deafening, possibly heard as far away as Fattoria.

The engineer tried frantically to stop the train by slamming on the brakes, but it was traveling way too fast. Suddenly it plunged through the breach with all cars still attached. It crashed on the bottom in a pile of smoke-covered rubble.

Fox team was Johnny-on-the-spot. Jack watched while they searched the rubble but there was no need. Not a one of them fired a shot. One of them waved and Enrico waved back. Then both teams began to scramble to put as much distance as they could between themselves and the explosion. It was a mission well planned and well executed. It was time now to go home and hole up while they waited for a new assignment.

Alfonso and Jack went back to the cave and the others returned to the lair. They were back in time to fix supper before it got dark.

Around nine that evening, Enrico and Vittoria rode in on the mules. By then, Alfonso and Jack had consumed more than just a little Dago Red. They poured cups for Vittoria and Enrico and waited for them to relax. Enrico lit up his pipe and took in a couple of draws. The suspense was driving Jack to distraction.

Finally, Enrico said, "Alante is ecstatic. He said to tell everyone they did a great job and in so doing, saved the lives of untold Italian citizens, including partisan foot soldiers such as we.

"The reports he's received so far indicate the SS company stationed outside Fattoria is in a state of high confusion which makes them extra dangerous. It also makes them vulnerable. Since they had a contingent of stormtroopers stationed inside the town and all civilian resident souls were accounted for, it was obvious even to the Krauts that no one there was involved in the explosion and derailment; however, that doesn't mean they won't make reprisals there to frighten the other communities in this sector.

"Right now, the SS company is under the temporary command of Oberleutnant (1st Lieutenant) Wilhelm Werner. He doesn't know what to do, so before a more senior officer arrives to take charge, we need to hit them again even harder. Since we've got plenty of dynamite left, plus two bazookas, Alante wants us to blow up their compound in the wee hours Sunday morning, August 1st. He doesn't believe they can get a replacement commander there that soon.

"You've all been there before, and we have accurate hand drawn maps. We leave tomorrow at 0800 to scout the area and devise a safe plan of action. I'm coming with.

"Get some sleep. This time the rest of us will come here to meet you for departure.

"Any questions? No? Good night."

Without further ado, he and Vittoria mounted the mules and rode back to the lair.

Chapter 10
Another Dangerous Mission

After they departed, Alfonso asked, "What are you thinking? I'm completely exhausted, not to mention a little drunk."

Jack responded, "Me too. 'No rest for the weary and the wicked don't need none.' Which are we - the wicked or the weary? Don't answer that.

"Back to our reality and this next mission. I hope the Krauts haven't had time to bulldoze our knolls. Also, we both know it. Alante's superior is right, whoever that is. The Krauts won't be expecting us - yet. We can obliterate the SS company stationed in Fattoria before they have time to regroup. This could be the decisive blow for us here in this sector of Sicily. The Americans and the Brits are driving the Krauts north off the island just we like we did in Africa. Maybe the Nazi slave masters will lick their wounds and decide to enslave the populace elsewhere. At least I hope so for our sakes."

Alfonso replied, "You're an undying optimist, Jack. I can hardly remember what it was like to live a normal life. You know. Not be crushed under the boots of our own Fascist leadership, not to mention the despicable Hun. This all started for us long before Der Fuhrer's blitzkrieg of Poland. It started back when Il Duce seized power. It won't end for us here in Italy unless we die or erase this pox called Fascism wherever it flourishes within our own people. Even if the Krauts move elsewhere, we will still be in a civil war with the Fascists. I see no end in sight, at least not for many more years.

"Sorry, I let my emotions get the better of me. How do you think we should blow up the Nazi compound to live to fight another day?"

"Keep the faith, brother. We plow on one step at a time. Don't lose heart. One day Italy will be free again and all because of folks like you and everyone else in Il Patrioti Invisibil. Knocking out the Nazi compound is our next step towards that goal. Right?"

"Right."

"Okay. When we were there to assassinate the top brass, I noticed that they didn't have any of those bloodthirsty German shepherd dogs they love so much. I'm hoping they still don't. Also, I only recall one manned guard tower, which was next to the front entrance on the south side. Do you remember if there was another one on the west side that we couldn't see?"

"There was not."

"Good. We'll have to doublecheck, but if there aren't any dogs or a second tower, this should be well within our capabilities. What we do is this. We have one bazooka team ready at our signal to knock out the tower. We cut the fence on the north side and slip an explosives team in. The building is about 18 inches off the ground so our team can slip in and set the charges underneath to blow the building to smithereens with all the enemy soldiers in it.

"Again, we'll have to check but I only recall two roving guards. They were patrolling individually around the compound, inside the fence in opposite directions. Is that also your recollection?"

"It is."

"If that hasn't changed, we're 'in like Flynn' - as they used to say about the movie star Errol Flynn and his scores of girlfriends.

This time Vittoria gets to play, too, but her role will be extremely dangerous. She'll need a backup nearby. She will also need to wear a dress and look slutty. From your previous missions, do you think she's truly capable of slitting an armed enemy's throat?"

"She is. Like me, she has her own demons driving her. She can do this."

"Good, because she has the most crucial role in my plan.

"We time the guards to see how long it takes for them to complete one circuit. Assuming the guards don't cross each other behind the building, we'll use Vittoria as a distraction to sidle up to them and slit their throats, first one and then the other. One of us will need to be in her hip pocket in a manner of speaking because we can't afford a shot being fired, waking up the entire compound. If that happens, our mission will have to be aborted, and we'll never have another opportunity like this again.

"After the first guard is eliminated, we drag his body under the building and wait for the next one to come around.

"We'll probably have two, maybe three minutes after that before the tower guards realize they haven't seen either patrol guard. They'll call in to the command post to send someone out to see why. At best, that will buy us one or two minutes more to set the charges and get out, so now I'm thinking we will need two explosive teams to set up the charges. However we decide to do it, the explosives teams need to be in and out in less than five minutes. They sneak back out of the compound the same way they went in.

"When we're out and ready to blow the charges, we signal the bazooka team, and it takes out the tower. Then we detonate the charges. At that point we can either slip away or stay to kill any survivors. However, if we plant the charges right there shouldn't be any.

"We won't have a lot of time to dilly dally around because they may still have a contingent of troops in town, but we should have at least three or four minutes and that's assuming the town SS are awake and dressed.

"If push comes to shove and Enrico wants, I could snipe them when they come running towards the compound. What do you think? Would it work?"

"Heck yeah! I'm glad you're on our side. It sounds perfect."

"I think so, pretty much. Timing is the key to success. I hope the Krauts haven't made any changes and that Enrico concurs."

"Me too."

The next morning, Saturday, July 31st, came around a little too early for Jack. He figured the others felt the same way because they'd been running on adrenaline for days on end. Nevertheless, they all understood the need for urgency. If they could knock out the entire SS compound including all the stormtroopers, maybe the SS command would decide to relocate the next detachment elsewhere out of Wolf's area of operations.

Wolf squad arrived on-site around 11 o'clock. The knolls were still there and intact. They watched and waited for the better part of an hour to see if there were any guards posted nearby that they couldn't see. Carlo climbed a tree and watched the compound from up on high. After he shimmied down, he said, "I didn't see anything of their usual activity. Except for the tower and the roving guards, not a stormtrooper was in sight. Weird."

They all pondered the lack of visible activity. No one came up with a viable theory.

Finally, Jack suggested, "Enrico, how about you let me do a

little scouting on my own? Pretty sure I can get up close undetected. Give me an hour to see what I can observe. Besides, if they do see me, they'll think the U.S. Army is nosing around and that'll put them all in a dither. Too bad we don't know where the American Army is. I wonder if they do. I'm pretty certain they haven't moved out of Sicily yet because there's too many German soldiers still here. I know the plan was to kill, capture, or drive them all out. I'll leave my hat here. That way they won't be searching for any partisans if they do spot me.

Enrico replied, "It sounds pretty dangerous to me and normally I'd say no. If anyone sees you get the heck out, but do NOT lead them directly back to us. If you can't get close enough to see anything, it's okay. We'll figure out something else."

"Roger that."

Jack slipped back into the woods behind them. When he was out of sight, he morphed into a sparrow. First, he flew to the west side of the compound to see if there was another gate or tower. There was not. Then he flew to the rear of the compound to examine the area he proposed breaching to Alfonso. It looked just like he thought. It had the same farm fencing with coiled barbed wire on the top that they could see from the knolls. Not only that, the area behind the compound going north towards Fattoria was brushy and afforded plenty of cover. Even better, this undeveloped area was not lit up at night by a lamppost.

He lit on a windowsill with an open window and morphed into a pesky housefly. He cruised inside. It looked like nearly all of the soldiers were seated in an auditorium getting a pep talk by Oberleutnant Werner on the benefits of being a diehard Nazi. Mind-numbing drivel, but the audience seemed to be gobbling it up like an ice cream sundae. Lip-smacking good!

Jack was surprised they weren't discussing war or military strategies or tactics or weaponry, etc. He counted 113 stormtroopers altogether, not including the three tower guards and the two rovers. He'd seen everything he needed to see here.

He flew back outside and morphed back into a sparrow. He flew to Fattoria 200 yards away. The citizens were going about their normal business. It was weird because he didn't see a solitary stormtrooper anywhere. He flew back to the woods behind the knolls and morphed into a rabbit and gorged himself on some lush green grass. Now all he had to do was come up with a plausible explanation as to how he ascertained so much intelligence in such a short period of time. Finally, he changed back into a soldier and walked back to the knoll where the squad was hunkered down.

He said, "It was surprisingly easy to get around because nearly all of the soldiers were indoors. I found a spot where I could watch the town. Everyone there appeared to be going about his regular routine. I didn't see the first Nazi there.

"Then I crept up to the fence behind the building. Their windows were all open, so I could hear everything which was being said. Also, I could see enough to determine that the men were seated in what appeared to be a large classroom. The oberleutnant was giving them what sounded like a political presentation, but my German isn't very good, so I'm not a hundred percent sure about that. Basically, I got the impression they were just killing time with mindless drivel, waiting for a new commander.

"The main thing is, what I overheard didn't sound like a bloodthirsty combat unit lusting for revenge like my old unit, The Big Red One, would have been doing. These really are political hacks dressed up like soldiers, even if they are supposed to be the most fearsome warriors alive. To me, they seem like the most brainwashed soldiers.

"So, what I ascertain is that they are in no way prepared for anyone to disrupt their dull, vulgar existence until a commander who knows what he is doing arrives and begins whipping them like the slaves they are.

"Oh yeah, there are no dogs on the premises. From what I could see, it looked like they have about a hundred troops altogether, give or take.

"Enrico, did Alfonso mention my rough draft proposal I suggested to him last night as to how we could blow this place up and send every last one of these Nazi supermen straight to perdition?"

"He did.

"First, good job on your scouting mission. Your timing must have been absolutely perfect and blessed by God above for you to get in and out unobserved with so much information. Either that, or you have a lucky rabbit's foot in your pocket.

"And second, yes, Alfonso did tell us, and we are all agreed. It's a great idea. The only problem is, Vittoria didn't bring a dress. Therefore, she's decided that once we cut the fence, she will leave her outer garments and shoes outside the fence line and approach barefoot in nothing but her undergarments like she's ready to meet her lover. Besides, she doesn't want to get blood on her favorite shirt.

"The plan is audacious, and we could really use three more people. We don't have them, so we'll have to make do. The key to this mission is to get the charges in place without being detected. In order to set the charges as quickly as possible, I've shifted things around just a little bit. See what you think.

"The bazooka team will be Carlo and Vittoria. Carlo will be the shooter. However, we will not set it up until after we've placed the charges and are ready to detonate. First things first.

"Alfonso, how many charges do we need; where do you propose we place them for maximum effect; and how long will it take?"

"Well, it's a two-story rectangular building about 50 meters long and 40 meters wide. The sleeping quarters except for command is on the second story. I'd say we use four-stick bundles since the construction is all wood. My suggestion is we place the charges in two rows lengthwise, with each row being 15 meters from each side of the building. Each row would begin five meters from the end and be spaced about 10 meters apart. That would be four charges per row times two, or eight total charges. If we had two, two-man teams, each setting one row, and we put in the fuses and strung the wire as we placed the bundles, we could probably have that all done in 20 minutes. We have to do this crawling on our backs which is why it will take so much time."

"That means we need to start wiring well before Vittoria distracts and kills the roving guards. How do we do that?"

Jack replied, "We make the least number of cuts possible on the fence on the lower portion closest to the ground. The teams go in and we make a temporary splice good enough to be unnoticeable so long as the fence doesn't sag and the guards aren't fixated on it. It'll be dark and if we don't make any noise they'll march right on by.

"When the teams are done and ready to come out, that's when we send in Vittoria, and only then if we think it's necessary. Our greatest fear after we come out is a guard noticing the wires leading to the detonator, which is why it probably will be necessary to kill them.

"We still have to time it but the guards probably cross paths every minute-and-a-half or so. Also, the guards probably switch out once an hour at the same time, so we'll need to time that, too. Assuming we don't kill the guards until after we've rigged the building, that's when the clock starts ticking. We'll have about three minutes for the bazooka team to get ready, synchronized as best we can with detonation."

Enrico responded, "Agreed. That leaves us with preparing our explosive charges, timing the guards and their relief schedule, and waiting for the bewitching hour. We'll take turns on watch, two at a time. Eat if you are so inclined. So long as the breeze is blowing in our direction, feel free to smoke until darkness befalls.

"Jack, you and I will take the first two-hour watch, followed by Vittoria and Carlo, followed by Benito and Alfonso. The time is 1330. We'll plan our engagement to begin between 0300 and 0330 unless we have to modify that based upon the guards' relief schedule. The same thing applies to the watchtower guards. One other thing. The guards need potty breaks, too. Happy thoughts."

While Jack and Enrico maintained the watch, they smoked and chatted quietly. Enrico said, "Benito could use a better gun. Right now, all he has is that double barrel, 12-gauge shotgun. If we can't come up with a suitable rifle, maybe we could at least come up with a handgun as a backup, and of course, the ammunition to feed it."

"I think we can accomplish that tonight. We should have two dead soldiers behind the building, both with a suitable rifle and hopefully with full ammo pouches. How about that?"

"That would be perfect. We'll grab them both and give Benito his choice. Let one of the others swap up if he wants or just keep it in the lair as a backup."

"If we don't blow up the tower too badly, we might even come up with a usable machine gun. Never know when something like that could come in handy."

"Jack, you're a scrounger deep in your heart but try not to get greedy. That bazooka will demolish the wooden guard tower and everything in it like it was made of matchsticks."

"'Waste not. Want not.'"

"Exactly, especially since we outfit and supply ourselves and don't have a steady revenue or supply stream. I noticed that you've decided to wear your American Army garb today. Why, I wonder?"

"I did. The clothes are more durable and fit me better. Also, I've been bringing all my gear with me because we're giant hunting and I never know if I'll survive to return to the outfit, or if we will need to hole up elsewhere. It's what the Army taught me to do. Be prepared. Also, Alante said he would send me back to the Army someday. Who knows when that will be?"

"He also said you were on probation and although he hasn't rescinded that, I'm pretty sure your probation is over. You're smart, loyal, tough, and an experienced warrior. The American Army isn't the only fighting unit happy to have you as a member of the team. Besides, I've noticed the sparks between Vittoria and you, although you both are exceptionally discreet. It's as obvious as the nose on your face."

"I won't deny it, but I'm 20 years her senior. Neither of us knows what the future will bring. Were this peacetime, I would do all I could to woo her and bind her heart to mine. As it is, all we have are strong 'what if' dreams. Maybe one day we could be lovers and even espoused to one another, but we both know it cannot be until the war is over. I pray her feelings will not fade after time because I know mine never will. I hope this conversation is in confidence. I would never do anything to sully her reputation. I just want her to be happy and fulfilled."

"Of course. My lips are sealed. Vittoria is like family to me, just like the others. I've noticed your discretion and think more of you for it. I do believe she would be fulfilled if the Good Lord above grants both of your hidden desires and wishes. I wish you both well."

"Thanks. Lord knows we need it."

During the lull, the squad determined that it took the guards nearly five minutes to make the circuit around the building. They were relieved on the hour in front of the building by the front steps. The tower guards appeared to be relieved every four hours, beginning at midnight. Everything the Germans did was precise and like clockwork.

At 2 o'clock Sunday morning, the squad left the knoll and sneaked up outside the wire on the back side of the building behind the bushes. Once again, they timed the guards. They decided they only had two minutes to get through the fence and crawl under the building without getting detected. They decided to wait until the 3 o'clock patrol went on duty.

After the first relief guard made his trek around the building, Enrico snipped the fence two feet from the bottom and three feet across. It was darker than Hades and the next guard passed by without noticing. As soon as he rounded the corner, Alfonso slipped under the wire toting a sack with four primed bundles of dynamite. He scurried under the building and waited. After the second guard passed, Carlo went out with a roll of wire. After the next guard passed, Benito slipped out with another tote full of bundles. He was followed by Jack with the wire. At 3:13, both teams were under the building and began crawling to the west end to set the charges. Tick tock. Tick tock. Besides sweating bullets, it was time for saying silent prayers.

At 3:34, Vittoria stripped down to her panties and camisole and slipped under the wire. She stood and pretended to look into one of the windows. She had her dagger clutched in her right hand out of sight. When the guard rounded the corner, she acted surprised and pretended she was going to try to slip back under the fence. The guard shouldered his rifle and grabbed her around the waist. That's when she shifted her body and jammed her knife deep into his heart. He fell without making a noise. Then Enrico slipped through the fence and helped Vittoria recover her dagger because it was stuck tight. He finally worked it loose, and together they dragged the stiff under the building. Then Erico grabbed the rifle and slipped back outside of the fence, pushing it together as best he could.

Vittoria's camisole was covered with blood so she took it off, wiped the blood off as best she could, and handed it to Enrico. All she had on were her panties. Then she poised herself like she was looking through the window.

She had just set up when the second guard came around the corner. She acted surprised and once again pretended she was trying to get back under the fence. This guard was stronger than the first and he pushed her to the ground face down. He ripped off her panties and began to unbutton his trousers to rape her, but when he rolled her over onto her back, she slashed this throat.

She was drenched with even more blood, so Enrico gave her his shirt to cover her up and so she wouldn't get blood on her favorite shirt. She slipped under the fence to get dressed where they had stashed their gear.

Then Enrico cut the fence up higher for the other guys to exit more quickly. He also took the second guard's rifle and stripped off both guards' ammunition pouches. It was 3:47, and time was of the essence.

Carlo was the first to crawl out from under the building. He turned around and gave Jack a hand and he crawled out. Then he helped Benito. Alfonso was last and he was trailing the wire.

They all ran back to where they had stashed their weapons, to include the bazooka and the detonator. Carlo picked up the bazooka and Vittoria grabbed the satchel of rockets. Enrico went with them as an overwatch. Jack and Benito stayed with Alfonso to cover him while he connected the wires to the plunger.

Just then a guard in the tower cranked up the siren, probably since they hadn't seen either roving guard for about ten minutes. Less than a minute later, Carlo fired a rocket into the tower and eliminated that threat, blowing it to pieces and obliterating the guards.

Alfonso pushed the plunger on the detonator, and the entire building went up in a blaze of fire, smoke, and debris. Not a soldier made it out of the burning inferno. They watched for several minutes before running back to the knolls and into the woods.

Mission accomplished, but it was an extremely close call for Vittoria.

This time they all went back to the lair. Alphonso cooked the ham. Carlo made the pancakes, and they all opted for Dago Red instead of coffee. Enrico departed the moment after he ate, riding Grazia over to speak to Alante.

Jack heated two buckets of water so Vittoria could wash up. Then all the men grabbed their chairs and sat out on the veranda so she could clean up while they smoked and drank more wine to unwind. When Vittoria was done washing, she joined them.

Jack could see she was terribly upset, but he had to keep quiet and sit on his hands. They all knew she had a close call and that they all owed tonight's success to her and what it had cost her in terms of her dignity.

Enrico didn't return until dawn. Part of his delay was the wait for two informers from Fattoria to show up with their observations of the destruction. Everyone was sitting on pins and needles. Nobody knew what to expect when the Nazis at SS headquarters in Messina learned about the loss of a second company of stormtroopers, plus their compound in Fattoria.

Alante said somebody from within their own intelligence group was reaching out for their U.S. Army intelligence contacts within either the 1st or 3rd Infantry Division, depending on who they could locate first. In the meantime, they were to stand down but remain alert.

What next?

Chapter 11
Wolf Squad Enjoys a Respite

The squad enjoyed 11 days of tranquility resting, playing games, and anything else which came to mind. Jack and Vittoria no longer pretended that they were anything other than sweethearts. You know what? It seemed that everyone in the squad already knew, and they were all happy for them. Jack and Vittoria spent all their waking moments doing everything together. Jack took her with him twice when he went deer hunting. He bagged two does four days apart and they all feasted like kings and one queen.

Then Enrico and Jack were summoned to go see Alante right away. Vittoria wanted to come along and of course, Enrico consented.

Alante greeted them all warmly. He said, "Sit down. What I have is mostly good news.

"You probably haven't heard yet, but the Allies have driven the Krauts all the way to Messina. They're trying to escape by ship across the Straits to the mainland, similar to the way the Brits escaped from them at Dunkirk. If they manage to pull this off, it'll be a bloodbath all the way up the mainland for months to come. However, once they're gone from Sicily, our war here will be all but over, and this is why.

"King Victor Emmanuel III recovered his throne and put Mussolini in jail. Not sure how that will work out yet, but I can't see Il Duce and the Fascists regaining control ever again. Most of Italy is sick to death of Mussolini and all his Fascist thugs. Also,

King Victor is supposedly engaged in meetings with the Allies to switch allegiance over to them. That would be a victory for Italy if he can pull it off.

"It also sounds like most of the Italian Army will remain faithful to the king with the exception of those traitorous units made up of hardcore Fascists. Already most, if not all, of those units have been splitting off and continue to fight with the Germans. Whichever way it goes, it's only a matter of weeks before Sicily will be completely rid of our German occupiers and hopefully all the Fascist units serving in our Army. Then life should get easier for us. Even so, we still need to be watchful of the Fascist sympathizers in our area and no doubt we will have orders to carry out a few more assassinations of the most egregious oppressors.

"Enrico, after Italy becomes an Allied nation, and the indications are it will happen within a few weeks, each member of Il Patrioti Invisibil will be given the option of returning home and taking up his old occupation or signing on with another likeminded group and continue the fight on the mainland.

"Tell all your squad members. Then let me know who wants to continue fighting and I will make the arrangements for them. And just so everyone is aware, as soon as the threat to Sicily is over, I'm done fighting. I long to return to my old teaching post at the university once again and I have been told I can. Until then, we will all continue to soldier on here in Sicily in the name of liberty, except for Jack.

"Jack, I called you here because time is of the essence and you need to repatriate with the 1st Division before they leave Italy. Rumor has it, they'll be leaving for England soon. If you don't join them before they embark, once the U.S. Army discovers you're still alive, you'll be branded as a deserter. Right now, as I understand it, you're listed as MIA (missing in action) since they never recovered your body.

"Jack, you are an honorable man, and you don't want to face a court martial, especially after all you've done for the cause of Italian liberation from the Nazis while you've been MIA.

"I've made arrangements with a Signore Adelmo Colombo to drive you and Enrico to Catania, where you both will board the train to Messina. At some point along the way, you should meet up with someone in the U.S. Army and get reunited.

"Our source tells me you should ask to speak with someone in your Military Intelligence section to debrief them on your exploits while you were with us. I'm sending a sealed letter with Enrico to give to them and that's why I'm sending him with you. It's so he can verify what you tell them.

"You both need to meet Signore Colombo at Dottore Rossi's house at 3 o'clock.

"Il Fantasma, you have been a tremendous asset to La Squadra dei Lupo and Il Patrioti Invisibil during your short tenure with us. I'm proud to have known you."

Alante rose and walked around his small table. Jack extended his paw to shake hands, but Alante came closer and embraced him Italian style in a bear hug. Then he said, "God willing, one day we will meet again when times are better. Now be off with you before you miss your ride."

Jack's head was spinning out of orbit. Now that he had finally found a charming, beautiful, and simpatico woman to love, he would be forced to give her up with a promise to resume at some nebulous date, hoping the fires would still be burning. It was all cascading like Niagara Falls, way too fast for him to swallow. The sand in the hourglass was rushing out and he couldn't think straight. For the first time in his life, he was a nervous wreck.

Vittoria said, "Enrico, I'm coming, too. I still have a dress, and I know how to act like a lady."

He replied, "But of course. You and Jack have much to discuss while we are on our journey."

Time was of the essence so while Jack collected his things, Enrico briefed Alfonso, Carlo, and Benito. They were all bursting with joy, juxtaposed with sorrow over the hasty departure of their new comrade, Jack.

Vittorio cleaned up. The only dress she still owned was simple, yet charming. It was cotton, mid-calf-length, with a full gathered skirt. It was white with small green and red designs and a strip of lace around the collar and the short sleeves. She put it on with her only pair of feminine footwear. She folded a few other garments and placed them with her toiletries and a few small keepsakes in the small valise she had carried when she fled Gela. It had been her mama's. Everything she had in it didn't weigh five pounds.

They made their hasty goodbyes and then left on foot for Hope.

Signore Colombo was standing by, dressed like a dandy and smoking a robust, black cigar. From the aroma, Jack knew it was a premium cigar, much better than his Certified Bond Blunts. Signore Colombo looked to be in his 40's, prosperous, and someone people did favors for, rather than someone who passed out favors. What did he owe Alante? He was impatiently waiting for them, standing next to his black, 1938, Fiat Model 1500 B, four-door saloon. It looked brand new, but of course it wasn't.

Jack wondered who Signore Colombo was and where he had

hidden his automobile from the Fascists. They exchanged pleasant greetings. The three amigos all placed their possessions in the trunk except for the rifles Enrico and Jack were carrying which they kept with them out of prudence. It was still too dangerous for a wayfarer to travel unarmed. The war had disrupted societal norms. It was difficult to ascertain who was friend and who was foe. Enrico rode in the right front seat and Jack and Vittoria sat in the back, glued together like Siamese twins.

Along the way Signore Colombo mentioned that the trip was about 100 kilometers (62 miles) and assuming they didn't encounter any difficulties, they would arrive no later than 6 o'clock. He planned to return home tonight. If they wished to stay to see Jack off, they would need to find another way back unless they were fortunate and encountered a U.S. Army officer at the train station. He would wait for them under those circumstances. (It was obvious to Jack that Signore Colombo had grudgingly assented to perform this taxi service because he was borderline grumpy and rude. He wasn't putting himself out any more than absolutely necessary. He must owe Alante big.)

Signore Colombo also said assuming the railroad schedule was still operating as usual, the next departure to Messina was at 8:14 p.m., arriving at 9:58. He said he'd made this very same trip many times. Of course, things could be delayed due to the fighting. Not only that, but he also didn't know if the Hun had torn up the train tracks in their retreat northward.

Signore Colombo despised the Hun. He had fought them in the Great War when he was a young man before he trained to be a lawyer. The Hun filled the air with poisonous gases when they attacked. That is an uncivilized way to wage war! It was sheer savagery using chemicals to annihilate their enemies. Bah! Look what they do to men, women, and children who are not combatants. They shoot and hang the innocents out of pure bloodlust. They're all animals!

Jack had to agree with him on this. Finally Signore Colombo calmed down. He and Enrico started a dialogue between themselves, affording the same opportunity to Vittoria and Jack. Soon the two lovers were so engrossed they forgot anyone else was in the car besides themselves.

Several miles outside of Catania as they were coming down a slight hill and rounding a curve, they saw a group of five or maybe six of what they initially assumed to be partisans about 300 yards away. They had set up a roadblock. Signore Colombo stopped the car to assess the situation, trying to decide what to do. The men had detained a passenger car with a man, two women, and three children. Suddenly, two of the partisans shoved the man on the ground and began kicking him. Two others went straight for the women and began fondling them. They watched in outrage as one of the men ripped the dress of one woman and was trying to disrobe her.

Enrico exclaimed, "The dirty scum! They're not partisans. They're Fascist bandits!"

Jack replied, "I can get two or maybe three of them before they can respond. Look! They have several horses tethered to the trees over there off to our front left. Enrico, I need you to cover me if any of them mount up and come charging towards us."

Enrico replied, "You've got it."

Both men disembarked from the sedan. Jack used the hood of the car to stabilize his aim. Bam! Bam! Bam! Within three seconds, the two men kicking the motorist dropped like swatted flies, as did another who stood by watching. Three bandits ran to the copse of trees next to their roadblock, mounted horses and rode off to the east. Who then, belonged to the horses tethered to their west?

Just then they heard horses galloping towards them from that direction. More bandits! Jack whipped around and dropped one with a shot through the heart. The other rider, armed with a pistol, shot Jack in the chest a split second before Enrico returned the favor and shot him dead.

Jack found himself lying on the ground face up. How did that happen? Signore Colombo scrambled to assist him. He said, "Lie still. Let me see how bad it is. Vittoria opened the trunk, bringing a small first aid kit plus the cloth bandage from Jack's ammunition belt.

Moments later Jack fainted from loss of blood. He didn't remember anything which happened after that.

In the meantime, the terrorized motorists Jack had just saved scrambled back to their dilapidated motorcar and skedaddled just as fast as the driver and his jalopy could muster.

Enrico exclaimed, "Help me lay Jack in the back seat. Vittoria, keep pressure on the bandage as hard as you can. We've got to get him to a doctor fast or he won't make it!"

Two minutes later they were on their way, motoring northbound too, just as fast as they could go. Catania was eight kilometers away. As they were approaching the outskirts, they were stopped at a checkpoint manned by American soldiers. The rattle trap Jack had saved was stopped there as well. The frantic driver began waving his arms and pointing at Signore Colombo's Fiat, explaining in broken English that these were the people who had rescued them.

"Enrico bailed out of the car and said, "Please, we have an emergency! The bandits shot an American soldier, and he needs medical attention fast or he will die!"

All it took was one look at Jack in his uniform for the soldiers to respond quickly. An officer named Captain Perkins took charge. He told them to follow him in his Jeep. Just before his driver sped off in a cloud of dust, he barked orders for some other soldiers to escort the other car to their command post for further interviews.

They took Jack to an Army MASH (Mobile Army Surgical Hospital) where he was rushed into surgery. Then Captain Perkins had Signore Colombo and party follow him to the MP (Military Police) office for further interviews. Upon arrival, they noticed that the carload of victims from the brush with the bandits was already in the process of being interviewed.

Enrico handed Captain Perkins the letter written by Alante. He read it and then began asking questions about Jack. Enrico provided everything he knew about Corporal John A. Rabbit of the 1st Infantry Division, stating how they encountered him on July 16th, and what all they had done since then in furtherance of the war against Germany.

Similarly, the MPs conducted separate interviews with Signore Colombo and Vittoria Bianchi, same as they had done with the carload of rescued citizens. This continued for several hours with more interviews, more questions, and finally, lengthy formal written statements. Immediately afterwards, the MPs escorted them to the mess hall and fed them, allowing them to eat and drink as much as they wanted. By then, the other carload of rescued citizens was long gone. It didn't seem like they were in trouble, but who knew? Vittoria was beside herself with grief and Enrico didn't seem much better.

They gorged on pot roast, green beans, sweet corn, carrot and celery sticks, fresh bread and butter, milk, stewed apples, and enough coffee to keep them awake all night. None of them had seen this much food at the same meal for years.

While they were enjoying one last cup of coffee, Captain Perkins informed them that they needed to remain overnight in temporary lodging until the information they provided could be verified. He thanked them for their service to the country, assuring them that they were not in any trouble and that they would be free to leave tomorrow.

In the interim, a soldier passed a note to Captain Perkins, stating that Jack was in critical condition but was expected to pull through. He relayed the good news.

The next morning, they were interviewed by a Major Taylor from the 1st Infantry Division's Military Intelligence command. He was specifically focused on Enrico since he was the squad leader for Wolf Squad. In that regard, he was especially interested in the assassinations of General Hoffman and Major Weber, the destruction of the troop train with all its passengers, and the destruction of the Nazi barracks with all inside. Of course, these were the three operations Jack had been involved with, and they were all game changers in southern Sicily. Major Taylor was profoundly impressed.

Enrico didn't know it, but the U.S. Army was already aware of these operations but hadn't a clue as to whom to express its appreciation. They were flabbergasted that one small squad with only six partisans (12 in the train mission) had the chutzpah to perform feats of such import and magnitude.

Later that day Jack regained consciousness, and though he

was heavily sedated, he was able to add more details. What none of the interviewers could understand is how he managed to survive his head injury during the amphibious landing at Gela, especially since two other soldiers in his platoon saw him get hit and fall beneath the surface of the water. How and why did he crawl to shore and beyond far enough away that the graves registration teams never found him?

All Jack could say was, "I don't know. I remember getting shot and I remember waking up in the woods several days later. I have no recollection of anything which occurred in between. Possibly some unknown party rescued me, not knowing my name and was subsequently killed. I wish I knew. Whoever it was, I owe him my life."

Then he asked, "Sir, will I return to the 1st?"

"No, Sergeant Rabbit. You will not.

"You will remain here at MASH until such time as you recover sufficiently and can be placed in a rehabilitation hospital here in Catania. Ultimately you will be transported back to the U.S. for any further rehabilitation after which you will be honorably discharged. "Travel to the U.S. will be space available on whatever transport we have at the time. It likely will be an American-flagged merchant vessel, but maybe not. It could be on an allied vessel. You won't know until we determine you're fit to travel on whatever ship we can find which has space.

"In the near future, the 1st will be departing to Jolly Old England and me along with it.

"You have several awards coming your way before we shuttle you back to the States along with other soldiers who are also being invalided out of the Army. Your records reflect that something similar to this happened to you in the Great War.

Remember that?"

"Yes, Sir, but you called me Sergeant. I'm a corporal, Sir."

"You were a corporal. You were promoted to sergeant today by order of Major General Terry, himself. He said to tell you congratulations on a job well done. He also said you will be receiving two oak leaf clusters for your Purple Heart and a second arrowhead device and a fourth battle star for your EAME. Something else may be in the works, too. You never know. I'll find out tomorrow. Not all good deeds go unpunished, Sergeant."

"Sir, what about the two men and the woman who brought me here? Can I see them?"

"They're still here. I'll make arrangements for them to come see you today before they return to Hope. I'll see you again tomorrow before I shove off with the rest of the Big Red One. Sergeant Rabbit, you're a credit to your family and to everyone else who has ever served in the 1st Infantry Division. See you tomorrow."

Later that day, Signore Colombo, Enrico, and Vittoria were ushered into the wardroom Jack shared with eight other patients who were recovering from surgery. An MP brought them in but said they could only stay for ten minutes.

Signore Colombo was brief. He said, "Jack, I'm very happy to hear you will make a complete recovery. It was nice meeting you. Thanks for saving our lives and the lives of those other unfortunate souls. Maybe one day we will meet again. Best wishes."

Jack replied, "Thank you, Sir, for bringing us here and for helping to save my life. I shall always be indebted to you. Have a safe trip home."

Enrico said, "Jack, you're a real hero. I feel fortunate that you came into our lives and did all the daring things you did and taught us about fighting a superior force. I know you're anxious to have a few moments alone with Vittoria. I just want to say that if you ever have the opportunity to return to Hope, I'd love to see you. Just so you know, my last name is Rizzo. Take care, my friend."

Jack responded, "The feeling is mutual. I wish things hadn't ended so abruptly. I hope, no matter what, that you will keep an eye out for Vittoria until we meet again. God speed."

"It goes without saying. Of course I will, as will the rest of our squad to the best of our abilities. Goodbye."

Assuming the MP was keeping a sharp eye on the clock, Jack only had five minutes left. He said, "Vittoria, I love you. How would you feel about getting engaged until we can sort things out? Er, that is, if you love me as much as I love you."

"Yes! I do love you that much, and more."

"Great! Now it's official. I need to find you an engagement ring."

"Zitto, amore mio. (Hush, my love.) Quickly, because our time today is short. I am staying here in Catania until it's time for you to ship out. I already found a job as a waitress and room and board with a sweet widow lady named Signora Angela Marino. Enrico and Signore Colombo are probably already on their way back to Hope by now.

"I heard you are being transferred to L'ospedale di Santa Maria, otherwise known to you Americans as Saint Mary's Hospital, maybe as soon as tomorrow. There are supposed to be 22 wounded Allied soldiers and sailors there already. Tomorrow I will check here first, and if you're not here I will check there. I will be working from 6 a.m. to 2 p.m. The name of the cafe is La Caffetteria di Lorenzo, or just plain Lorenzo's. Anyone here can tell you where it's at."

"Do you have money? I have more than a year's worth of wages that I've hardly touched. It's hidden in my pack."

"No, but I may need some if my job doesn't work out. Look, I will see you tomorrow afternoon when we have more time. I must go. Ti amo."

She squeezed his hand and kissed him on the lips. Then she turned to leave.

Jack replied, "I love you, too."

Jack thought to himself. Even the native civilians know more about what the Army is doing than its soldiers do! Sheesh!

The MP came over to escort her out, but Vittoria was already skipping out of the ward, flying high on Cloud 9.

The following morning, Major Taylor returned, and he brought an Army photographer with him. They gussied up Jack as much as they could. Then the photographer took several snaps of Jack receiving the Legion of Merit from Major Taylor. It had been awarded by orders of Major General Terry for the three significant clandestine operations he had conducted with the Italian Royalist partisans after he was wounded during the Battle of Gela. When the ceremony was over, Major Taylor handed him a copy of the citation order signed by Major General Terry and the fancy blue and gold-trimmed box the medal came in.

Major Taylor said, "Be careful Sergeant, when you open the box. It also has your second arrowhead device and your fourth battle star for your EAME, plus two oak leaf clusters for your Purple Heart. In addition, they didn't do this when you received your Bronze Star, but yours was for valor, so now we pin a V-device for valor on it. General Taylor wanted me to be sure and tell you that, and that he's extremely proud of you and your service to God and Country. He wishes you the best life has to offer."

"Thank you, Sir. Please pass my gratitude along to General Terry."

They exchanged salutes, and Major Taylor made his exit.

Three weeks later, Jack's photograph receiving the Legion of Merit was featured in the *Stars & Stripes* newspaper. The whole world saw it - even sister Phoebe and Cousin Gerard, both of whom purchased several copies of it for posterity. Jack gave his copy to Vittoria.

Chapter 12
Healing and Making Plans

On Saturday, August 14th, Jack and a 22-year-old sailor named Herbert F. Towers, a Seaman 1/c from Detroit, Michigan, who now was stabilized from shrapnel wounds sustained in the Battle of Gela, were both transported to St. Mary's Hospital. Towers was a pretty good kid. He wasn't sure yet if he would regain full use of his right arm. Jack reckoned it was a good thing the kid was a southpaw.

They were lodged on the 2nd floor in a 6-man ward which until now only had one patient. His name was Pfc LaRue R. Boyd, from Jackson, Mississippi. He was a Sherman tank driver in the 1st Armored Division whose tank was clobbered by a panzer. He managed to escape out the bottom hatch. The other three men in his crew didn't make it. Boyd was suffering from a severe brain injury caused by the concussion. His mind was still addled. The doctors didn't know if he would ever recover. They were hoping.

Vittoria found Jack about 3:30. It was a mile walk from the MASH unit where she went first before checking St. Mary's. At least the visiting hours were from noon until 8 o'clock here. When the hospital was jam packed, they ran the visitors off after a 2-hour visit. Today was not a busy day, so she was able to stay substantially longer.

Jack still wasn't ambulatory except for unsteady trips to the latrine, but he was getting stronger. (He despised using a bedpan.) On one hand, he didn't want to heal too rapidly and cut short his time with Vittoria. On the other hand, he was hatching a plan to get her to America with him. There were a number of things they needed to accomplish first to make that possible.

Vittoria wasn't aware of Jack's ruminations on this matter until after she arrived, nearly out of breath after her long walk at a spooked ostrich's pace. No sooner had she entered the room when he asked without even saying hello, "If I can pull it off, will you come to America with me?"

Somewhat astonished, she replied cheerily, "Of course, you silly rabbit! (Did she know, or was this just a pet name she had for him due to his surname?) Don't you know most downtrodden people and nearly everyone whose lover is from over there would like to live in America? It's just that I don't know how you could possibly arrange it. I'm afraid of getting my hopes up, only to see them dashed to pieces when you leave without me."

"I won't leave you behind. Do you have your birth certificate?"

"Of course I do. I can bring it to you tomorrow if you want to see it."

"Well, that's Step 1. Do you know what a Questura is?"

"No."

"Well, I do. It's an office at any police department headquarters in Italy where a person goes to apply for a passport."

"How do you know that? I never heard of it."

"You don't need to know about it unless you need a passport, amore mio."

"Why are you asking me all these questions? Is it not enough to know that I love you?"

"It was until I started asking questions so I can figure out how to get you into America legally. Now who's the silly rabbit?"

"Oh my gosh! You're really serious about this! Now my heart is pounding like I nearly fell off a cliff."

"Come here and let me kiss you and make it all better."

"Your roommates will see me and think I'm a loose woman."

Nevertheless, she looked around and saw that one was sleeping, and the other was reading a newspaper printed in English. She tiptoed over and gave him a kiss like one would expect from his sister or spinster aunt, so he raised up in the bed (painfully) and stole a proper kiss. She smacked him playfully on his cheek and sat down in the visitor's chair out of his reach.

She whispered, "What if they saw me?"

"Then I would tell them you are my fiancé."

"Shush. Tell me more about your plan. I'm all ears, Sergeant Rabbit." (Another joke, he hoped.)

"Monday after work, take your birth certificate to the police department and ask for the Questura. Then make an application for a passport. Hopefully, it won't take much time or cost too much. Let me know. I'll gladly pay whatever they ask. This is the easiest part of my plan."

"Which is what exactly?"

"To take my wife to America with me."

"But I'm not your moglie. Do you even know what that is?"

"Yes. It means wife, but you will be if you want to be. We need to talk about that too."

"Please continue. Don't leave anything out. I'm feeling breathless again."

"Well, I know you're a Catholic, but I'm a Protestant - a Presbyterian in fact although I attend the Baptist Church because it's much closer. Truth is, I don't care if you remain a Roman Catholic until the day you die, but a Catholic priest would never consent to marry us because he would consider me a pagan. We could marry civilly at the local city or county clerk's office without clergy; however, to have a religious ceremony we will need to find a Protestant clergyman.

First problem is, I don't know if you would consent to do that, and the second problem is, I don't know if there are any Protestant preachers in Italy, let alone here in Catania."

"Silly rabbit, of course I will marry you, even if the ceremony is conducted by a county clerk or a Jewish rabbi. And yes, there is a small Chiesa Cristiana Protestante here in Catania. The pastor's name is Reverendo Leonardo Giordano. When you are ready, I will go speak with him. We can marry there."

"Perfect. That's one of the thousands of reasons I love you, Vittoria. First, though, let's get you a passport. Then we marry, because the next two steps are a little trickier.

"How so?"

"First you must possess a passport, a document in which the Italian government affirms that you are who you purport to be.

"Next, you will need to obtain a visa issued by the U.S. government. It allows you to enter the country for a specified period of time. It's either a piece of paper they give you or a stamp they put in your passport. I've never seen one, so I'm not sure which. I just learned about them.

"There are several types of visas, and they have an expiration date by which you must leave the country. We can rectify that when you apply to become naturalized as a U.S. citizen, but first you need to gain legal admittance, meaning you must obtain a visa. The main thing is that the visa allows you to enter America. I don't know yet where we would apply for a visa here, but I'm working on it.

"There are three types of visas that I know of. The first is a tourist visa which is the easiest to obtain but it's only good for a short stay.

"Another is a work visa which is easier to get approved if the applicant already has a guaranteed job lined up. I could make that happen through my friend, Woodrow Falstaff, who owns a general store about a mile from me, but it might take some time to get it approved.

"The best way is if you apply as a dependent of an American citizen which opens the door to become a naturalized citizen after you're in the U.S. This is what I'd like to do, just as soon as we obtain a marriage license.

"The other obstacle is that as a soldier, I'm supposed to get permission from my commander before I marry. Some commanders are dead set against granting permission, particularly as it relates to 'war brides'. I'm hoping my new commander doesn't feel that way, especially since they're going to discharge me as soon as I recover anyway. The other problem is I don't know who my new commander is! The 1st Infantry Division is no longer here in Italy. They went to England. Now I'm attached to an administrative unit awaiting discharge. Hopefully once I meet him, he won't have any objections.

"Of course, I could always get married without asking permission but I'm not sure how that would play out when you apply for a visa. Not only that, they could court martial me although I don't think they would.

"The final part of my plan is to get you booked on the same vessel they will send me home on. The obstacle there, is that I don't know when that will be or which ship it will be. I probably won't find out until the ship is in port and that could be from any of the coastal cities in Sicily.

"Worst case scenario is you might have to travel on a different ship. However, once you have a visa you can depart whenever we can arrange it."

"What do you think?"

"There are so many ifs, not to mention how could we afford it my love? I don't know how much a ticket to go to America would cost, but it's bound to be quite expensive. Of course I'm game. I've never been on a ship before. It would really be fun, especially if we were on the same ship but the more I understand the procedure, the less confidence I have we can accomplish it."

"I was going to tell you this the other day, but we ran out of time. Since I've been in the Army, which is 21 months now, I've hardly spent any money. I've saved nearly all my wages.

"I haven't checked, but I'm certain we could book your passage for less than $300 and I can afford that and still have plenty left over. Heck, as long as we're in Italy, the exchange rate is 120 liras to the dollar, and I have no overhead. It's cheap for me here so long as the Army is paying me.

"I would stay here to be with you but they're going to ship me back home no matter what I want. I don't have a passport or a visa even if they would let me stay. Besides, it's not much but I already own a cabin, 160 acres of farmland, plus a mule and a dog that Cousin Gerard is caring for in my absence. I love living there and I think you would, too."

"Jack, I would follow you to Siberia if I had to in order to be with you. Even so, I would much prefer living in Kentucky with you. From your description, it is beautiful, and the farmland is rich.

"My family is gone. I have no money to speak of, no house

because Papa rented the house we lived in, nowhere to call my own, plus I love you with all my heart. I want to be with you. My fear has always been that it would never come to pass for any number of reasons - that it's just a dream like 'pie in the sky'. You can't begin to imagine how much I want this."

"I can imagine, because my family consists of my cousin and his family, who live a half mile from me, and my sister, who lives more than a thousand miles away. Not only that, I love you like I've never loved anyone before. I never want our time together to end.

"I feel certain I can make this work. Now you know what must be done to make it so."

She ran over to his bed and fell across his chest, weeping like he'd never seen anyone do before. It was terrifying. He did not know how to comfort her.

Finally, she composed herself and said, "I thank God every single day for bringing us together. I'm all in until death do us part."

That put a smile on his face Father Time couldn't erase.

The rest of their time together that afternoon passed in harmony and ended much too soon. Vittoria stayed with him while he ate what an orderly brought him for supper. It consisted of meatloaf, mashed potatoes, English peas, bread and butter, peach cobbler, and iced tea. He even brought Vittoria a meal, first because he was a very nice man, and second because the Americans were picking up the tab and they had no shortage of food.

Vittoria returned at noon on Sunday. This time she brought him some applesauce cookies Signora Marino had baked. They were oh so yummy. It was the Sabbath, so everything was closed.

Jack couldn't go anywhere anyway, so they spent the afternoon talking about the future and lining up what they needed to do to get her to America. It was time well spent.

Monday morning Jack asked his Navy roommate if he knew the name of the commander of the U.S. military detachment there in Catania. He replied that he thought it was an Army major in the quartermasters by the name of Edwards. He knew Colonel Dunbar was the doctor in charge of the MASH unit, and he was pretty sure Major Edwards was in charge of everyone else who was stationed there. He was responsible all U.S. military personnel who were not part of MASH, housing, supplies, vehicles, transportation, contracts with the locals, and absolutely everything else the doctors didn't want to be bothered with.

"Do you know where his office is located?"

"Well, I heard they took over a bank building that was shut down a year or so ago. It's a two-story brick building. Used to be called Farmers Bank - in Italian, of course. Supposedly there's a new sign which says U.S. Army Command. It's a couple of blocks down from the hospital on the same side of the street. One of the orderlies told me."

"Have you seen any American soldiers here in the hospital who aren't hospitalized or assigned to MASH? Was the orderly you spoke with a soldier? What was he wearing? Was he even an American?

"Hmmm. Not sure, but I think so. I do understand that soldiers assigned to Major Edwards come once every day or so checking on things under their control, such as the food we eat and the care we receive. They also pass out letters addressed to patients who've been here for awhile, collect letters to be mailed home, and also check to find out who needs to be shipped out.

Why the sudden interest?"

"You saw my fiancé yesterday. Her name is Vittoria. I want to get married and take her back to the U.S. I need his permission."

"Do you have the dough to do it? I heard it costs about $300 to book passage back to the States. At least that's what I was told the going rate is to ship us back on a commercial vessel soon as we're well enough to go. That's a whole lotta moola. About six months' pay, I'd say. Were you born rich or something? You own a printing press? How did you ever get that much jingle? You win a poker game before you was wounded?"

"No, but I've got the money. I've saved most of my pay. Nowhere to spend it when you live in a foxhole. Anyway, Vittoria's applying to get a passport this afternoon, but she also needs a visa, and I think that's done through the U.S. State Department. Do you think they have anyone here in Catania?

"Good question. I don't know, but Catania is supposed to be the largest city in Sicily. If anyone from the State Department is assigned to Sicily, I'm sure they're in Catania. Problem is, we're at war with Italy, don't cha know? I don't think you could find any non-combatants here. The Fascists would have deported them or put them in jail. At least that's the way I figure it.

"Where's your fiancé from?"

"Gela, but the Nazis wiped out her family, so she moved to a small village in the same general area that nobody ever heard of before. It's called Speranza. It means Hope. She was a member of a loyalist partisan group who found me after I was wounded in the Battle of Gela. She's fought the Fascists and Nazis as fiercely as anyone."

"Well, if she can prove it, I bet they'll issue her a visa."

"She can prove it all right. She was on three guerrilla missions with me. Other members of the same group still reside in vicinity of Speranza."

"Well, you receiving the Legion of Merit and all those Purple Hearts, if you marry her, I bet they'll give her a visa, but you gotta get permission to marry her first. Pretty sure that will be up to Major Edwards"

"Agreed. That's why I need to see him - to ask for permission."

"Next time one of the boys from Major Edwards' department comes by you need to hit him up. How long do you think you'll be here in recovery?"

"Maybe a month. I think I should be healthy enough by then unless I get an infection."

"What kind of a job do you have back home?"

"I'm a farmer. I've got a quarter-section in Eastern Kentucky."

"You own 160-acre farm?"

"I do. It was my daddy's. All of my family except for my older sister died in an electrical storm a number of years ago, so now the farm belongs to me. My cousin is farming it for me until I return."

"Lucky dog. You know what I own?"

"What?"

"The clothes and tools in the closet of my daddy's house. I used to be an auto mechanic, but now I don't know what I am. What will I do if I can't work?"

"You're a disabled vet who put it all on the line for his country, but you can't think like that. You gotta keep exercising that right arm. It'll get better. Don't give up hope. Where there's a will there's a way."

"You know, I actually thought about making a career in the Navy, but now that I'm all bunged up, they're gonna toss me out on my ear. A Purple Heart is supposed to make it all okay. It's real nice and I'm appreciative, but it's not all okay."

"Well, did you ever consider the U.S. Merchant Marine? I bet you could get on with them. They pay really well too - a whole lot better than the Navy. Of course, the U-boats make that a really hazardous way to earn a living. Probably have to sign on as an ordinary seaman. That's the bottom rung on the ladder."

"Listen to who's talking - a volunteer Army infantryman! I'll take my chances on a ship any day, but I never thought of the Merchant Marine. That's a great idea. I might even get a ship on the Great Lakes. Besides, I've been low man on the totem pole most of my life. Maybe I will. I'll check it out. I love being at sea. I'll ask the orderly when he stops by to see if we want to check out a book if they have any on the Merchant Marine."

"That's the ticket. Herbie, you know I wish you all the best. Whatever you do, don't ever give up."

"You bet. One day I'll make my mark."

Chapter 13

Pulling Together Like a Team of Mules

Later in the day, a soldier stopped by, checking on the welfare of the patients, collecting and passing out letters, and dropping off a copy of the *Stars and Stripes* newspaper in each ward.

Jack asked, "What's your name, soldier, and what unit are you in?"

"My name is Pfc Caleb Ellis, Sergeant. Nice to meet you. I'm a member of the 2431st Quartermaster Battalion, headquartered here in Catania. We support the MASH and all the troops convalescing until they're shipped back to the States, or for a few, return to their units. What can I do for you, Sergeant Rabbit?"

"Call me Jack. Where do you call home, Caleb?"

"Bowling Green, Kentucky, Sarge. You probably never heard of it."

"I have. I'm from a small town in Lawrence County in Eastern Kentucky. Glad to make your acquaintance, by the way."

"Geez, Sarge. It's a small world. Can I get you anything? Do you have a letter you'd like to mail?"

"Not today. If you can get me a few envelopes and some paper and something to write with, I will have two letters if you come back tomorrow."

"Coming right up." He reached into his satchel and produced a small stationery tablet, a packet with six envelopes, and a yellow number two pencil. "Anything else?"

"Yes. Is Major Edwards your commander?"

"Sure is. Major Enos K. Edwards. Smokes a corncob pipe like General MacArthur. Likes horse and automobile racing. Daddy was a pharmacist who sold more pints of bourbon than medicine, with a prescription of course, back in the day when it was only way you could buy it legally due to Prohibition. Major Edwards went to Marshall University on a basketball and a track and field scholarship. Swell fellow. Used to be the postmaster in Wheeling, West Virginia before the war started. He's in the Army Reserves and they activated him. Said he's going back and pick up where he left off soon as we win this war. Married and has four girls. No boys. You'd really like him."

"How can you possibly know all this about him?"

"Everyone in the detachment knows. He stays involved in everything we do. Talks to everybody. All the fellers love him. His open-door policy is not just lip service. It's real.

"Captain Broussard's our XO (executive officer). He's a good feller too, but don't say much. Heard he was from Maine up on the Canuck border. Also heard his daddy and he own a general store which is the onliest one around for 50 miles. Probably so far back in the woods you learn to speak bear, so you at least got something to talk to. He ain't married so far as I know. Oh, I do know something else about him. He's a Distinguished Rifle Marksman. Competes in the Camp Perry National Matches, at least he used to before the war. All the other officers carry a .45 pistol, but he carries an M-1 carbine like us enlisted guys. He said he'd rather have the M-1 Garand, but they don't issue them to the quartermasters. I heard he made some alterations on his to make it more accurate."

"Caleb, you are a fountain of information, as well as a great public relations man for your unit. Kudos to you. If I write a note to Major Weber asking him to stop by and see me, would you give it to him for me?"

"Sure would. Tell you what. Sarge, you write the note while I finish my rounds. I'll stop by on my way out when I get done and pick it up. Probably be about an hour."

"Thanks. In that amount of time, I'll probably also have a couple of letters to go."

"All righty then. Be back."

Jack got busy and wrote a short note to Major Edwards. It read, "Sir, at your convenience, could you stop by the hospital and give me a few moments? I have something of great importance to me which I need to discuss with you. Sincerely, Sergeant John A. Rabbit, August 16, 1943." He also wrote a short letter to both Cousin Gerard and Sister Phoebe. When Pfc Ellis completed his rounds, he picked them up.

Vittoria stopped by at 3:30. She was all smiles. She reported that she had applied for a passport. It was easier than she had imagined. It only cost 230 Liras, and it would be ready for her to pick up on Friday.

While she was visiting, Major Enos K. Edwards and his orderly, Corporal Leon F. Turnipseed, stopped by. Jack was astonished that Major Edwards had responded this quickly.

Major Edwards introduced Corporal Turnipseed. Jack introduced his two roommates, Seaman 1/c Herbert Towers, followed by Pfc LaRue Boyd, who was sleeping. Just as he was about to introduce Vittoria, Major Edwards asked, "And who is this charming lady?"

Vittoria curtsied and replied, "Major, my name is Vittoria Maria Bianchi."

Major Edwards smiled. He shook her hand by the tips of her

fingers and exclaimed, "But of course! You're the brave young lady I read about in the letter written by a leader in the resistance that Sergeant Rabbit served with for a short while. I'm honored to meet you, Miss Vittoria."

Vittoria blushed bright red and smiled. She said, "Thank you, Sir. I'm honored to meet you as well."

Then Major Edwards said, "I may know what this is about. Sergeant Rabbit, do you wish to have a private meeting with me, or would it be okay if everyone else stayed?"

"Sir, it's okay if everyone stays.

"Sir, Vittoria is my fiancé, and we want to get married. I want to bring her back to America with me when I go. I have the money to pay for her passage. Today Vittoria applied for a passport, but I know she will still need to get a visa. I'm not sure how to go about that. First though, I beg your permission for us to wed."

Major Edwards looked over to Vittoria and asked, "Miss Vittoria, is this true? Do you love Sergeant Rabbit with all your heart and wish to become his lawfully wedded wife?"

She erupted into tears and replied, "Yes! Yes! With all my heart and strength and being."

He smiled and handed her a tissue to wipe her eyes. Then he said, "Sergeant Rabbit, you have my permission. I will also help you to secure the visa, but first I want to ask Miss Vittoria a question."

"Yes, Sir. Anything."

"Regarding the mission to blow up the Nazi barracks, were you the young woman who was assigned to eliminate the guards, and in fact did it?"

She blushed bright red. "Yes, Sir. That was I."

"Remarkable! How did you summon the courage?"

"Sir, there were only six of us against more than a hundred. This had to be done so we could detonate the charges and escape. I almost got overwhelmed by the second guard, but our squad leader, Enrico Rizzo, was hidden and would have saved me had I been unable to help myself. Sir, the SS came into my papa's house and murdered him and my mama and two brothers while I was elsewhere. You know why? Because a Fascist informer told them papa was passing information to the Allies! I hope you won't think less of me now that you know this about me."

"Of course not! It impresses me even more. What strength of character you have! What you did that night was certainly worthy of a Bronze Star Medal. Unfortunately, it takes a lieutenant colonel or higher to award that. However, what I will do is award you an Army Commendation Medal with a V device for valor. That should be all the reference you will ever need besides Sergeant Rabbit as your sponsor to get the State Department to grant the visa.

"Sergeant Rabbit, when you have a wedding date, let me know and I will attend as a witness to the ceremony. Afterwards, when Miss Vittoria is ready to apply for the visa, let me know and I'll contact the right person at State. There's just one here, and he has an office in our building.

"The only other matter is your passage to the U.S."

"I spoke with Colonel Dunbar. He said your recovery is coming along nicely. He thinks you can be released in about four weeks. That puts us in mid-September. We try not to use ports along the Mediterranean Sea because of Nazi submarines. I will let you know in plenty of time when and where and which vessel, so you can make the arrangements for Vittoria. In fact, I'll make sure Captain Broussard notifies the shipping agent that Vittoria will need a berth, too.

"Anything else?"

Jack replied, "No, Sir. You covered everything. We are so indebted to you. Thank you very much, Sir."

Vittoria asked, "Major Edwards, Sir, will you give me away? My poor papa is no more." She was gushing tears like Old Faithful and shaking like she was freezing cold.

He answered, "It would be my honor. Be here Wednesday afternoon at 3:30, all dressed up, and we'll hold your award ceremony. Bring anyone you like as a witness. In the meantime, line up your preacher and set a date. You have much to do. Let's get this show on the road. Time is a wasting."

After Major Edwards and his orderly, Corporal Turnipseed departed, Herbie said, "Dern, Sarge, your problems are solved. You got a beautiful woman soon to be your wife, and afore long, you'll be back in your cabin, snug as a bug in a rug. Congratulations, you two! Think he could help me find a job in the Merchant Marine?"

Jack replied, "Why don't you jot a note to him and ask when he returns on Wednesday? By the way, how's that right arm coming along?"

"I think it's gonna be okay."

"Excellent. Think how you want to phrase your request. Get it right before you ask."

"I will. Thanks."

On Wednesday, Major Edwards returned with a photographer and a reporter from the *Stars and Stripes* newspaper. He presented the award to Vittoria, pinning it on her dress. Then a couple of orderlies wheeled in a cart covered with cupcakes and pitchers of fruit punch. It was a festive occasion for all who were present, which turned out to be about a dozen altogether, mostly hospital orderlies and Vittoria's landlady, Signora Marino. Vittoria was overwhelmed with emotion and had a hard time trying to curb her tears.

Friday Vittoria obtained her passport. In the interim, she went to the Protestant Christian Church and met Reverendo Leonardo Giordano. He was a short, bald, plump, 40-ish friar, who left the Roman Catholic Church before the war began because he wished to marry a Protestant woman. Of course, the Roman Catholic Church said no, so he left the order. Marry he did, and then he got ordained as a non-denominational Christian minister.

The rotund clergyman was energetic, friendly, and a deeply compassionate man of God. He was empathetic to Vittorio's request. She brought him to the hospital to meet her betrothed the very next day. He and Jack bonded quickly. As soon as he determined they were committed to each other until death do them part, and that Major Edwards consented to the marriage, he was on board.

He asked, "Sergeant Rabbit, when do you think you would be well enough to stand before God in our humble chapel in order to be wed?"

"Not sure yet Sir, but I believe I could do it within two weeks. I'll ask Colonel Dunbar if he would consent to my absence long enough for me to get married on my feet. I truly hope I don't have to marry while I'm confined to my bed."

"Vittoria, as soon as your fiancé has an answer, come see me and we'll set a time and date and make all the arrangements, okay?"

"Sí, Reverendo Giordano. Grazie."

The following day, Jack asked the attending nurse, 1st

Lieutenant Helen Doyle, if she would ask Colonel Dunbar to stop by and see him. She replied, "Well he's an awfully busy man. Why do you want to see him?"

"Have you seen the young lady who comes to visit me every afternoon?"

"You bet. She's very beautiful. Everyone here has seen her."

"Her name is Vittoria Bianchi. She's my fiancé. Major Edwards has granted us permission to marry. Reverend Giordano has said he will officiate. I want to get married in his church instead of in the hospital ward. All I need is a couple of hours. I was wondering when he thought I would be well enough to stand long enough to do that."

"Oh, my gosh! This is fabulous! Congratulations! But Sergeant, how will you get her to the U.S.? It's got to cost several hundred dollars! She would need a visa! You'd have to move mountains to pull this off."

"I've got the money. Major Edwards said he would get her passage on the same vessel that takes me back to America. As soon as we are wed, he will assist us in procuring a visa for her."

"Wow! You've thought this completely through and worked it out. What will you do after the Army discharges you?"

"I have a 160-acre farm back home in Kentucky. We'll grow corn and raise chickens, and maybe a few head of cattle. All I have to do is get Vittoria back there with me."

"The Lord knows you deserve it after three Purple Hearts and the Legion of Merit.

"I'll speak with Colonel Dunbar for you and see what he says. He probably won't come over to see you personally, but I would be happy to convey whatever his answer is. Truthfully, I think you could do this in a week or two, but we'll see what he says.

Good luck!"

The following day, Lieutenant Doyle told Jack that Colonel Dunbar said Jack needed two more weeks before he could stand long enough to marry. That put it up to August 31st. She said he could marry any time after then. Then Lieutenant Doyle dropped a bombshell on him.

She said, "They want to shut down operations here in Sicily as soon as possible and move to the mainland. They're going to ship out all our patients who are well enough by September 15th. I don't know how long it takes to get a visa for your fiancé, but you need to get Major Edwards to shake a leg. What I'm saying is, you better marry as quickly as you can arrange it if you want to travel to America on the same ship."

"Thanks, Lieutenant. I owe you big time. I'll jump right on this."

That afternoon when Vittorio stopped by Jack told her what he had learned. He told her to line up the wedding for Wednesday afternoon, September 1st. He also handed her a note to pass along to Major Edwards on her way home this evening. They only had two weeks from their wedding day to secure her visa and make arrangements for her to sail with him. The only other option was for them to wed right away in the hospital. Vittoria said she would ask Major Edwards what to do.

Vittoria did not linger. She took the note, kissed Jack with pent up passion, and hurried over to Major Edwards' office. He was still there, and of course, he had time for her.

He read the note, and said, "Congratulations on setting your wedding date. I will be there to give you away.

"Everything will work out fine. I've spoken with Mr. Vincent T. Caruso from the U.S. State Department, and he's assured me that as soon as he sees your marriage certificate, he will issue the visa. Also, we've been expecting this transfer to the mainland, so Captain Broussard's already working on transportation for at least 40 troops, plus you, to the States. Your passage will cost $274.00, same as we pay for our troops, and he assures me he can get you both on the same vessel.

"It's too early to know the name of the vessel. If we can, we'd like to book everyone through Trapani to New York City; however, the trip to Trapani from here is two days by rail, which is another $12 for you. That being said, we may decide to ship from Gela, simply because the train ride is shorter, and the men we are shipping home are still recovering from their wounds. The travel would be difficult for many of them. At least they'll have a berth on the ship, just as soon as we can get them to the port.

"I hope this puts your heart at ease."

"It does. Thank you, Sir.

"Sir, Jack does not have a uniform he can wear."

"Tell him I'll send someone from Quartermaster Supply to see him tomorrow. His kit with everything he had here has already been shipped to his home address. It should be there waiting for him when he returns.

"Anything else?"

"No, Sir. Thank you."

"Don't worry. This will all work out."

Vittoria raced back to the hospital to give Jack the good news.

Time slipped by quickly with notice by everyone in the hospital. Everyone had much to do before they departed Catania. Nevertheless, things fell into place. Jack was getting stronger. He could walk short distances. He wrote letter after letter to Phoebe and Gerard. So far, he had yet to receive a reply, but he hadn't expected one. Still, he hoped.

September 1ˢᵗ was a beautiful day. Major Edwards walked Vittoria down the aisle. She was wearing the new dress Signor Angela Marino, her landlady, stitched for her by hand. It was white cotton, open around the neck and shoulders, calf-length, with lots of eyelet lace. Vittoria looked radiant.

Jack was wearing his new uniform with the short waisted Ike Jacket. All his medals were in his belongings, except for his Legion of Merit, so that's all he pinned on until Major Edwards gave him another Combat Infantryman's Badge.

Reverendo Leonardo Giardino performed the ceremony, short but sweet. They enjoyed a small reception afterwards in the basement. A photographer assigned to the 2431ˢᵗ Quartermaster Battalion took several photographs, which Major Edwards later presented to Vittoria. Mr. Caruso from State Department was present and after the ceremony he presented Vittoria with her visa.

Jack was exhausted so he and Vittoria returned to the hospital courtesy of Mr. Caruso and his black Mercedes Benz sedan which had been seized from the Fascists.

It was done. Now they waited impatiently to go to America.

Chapter 14

Mr. & Mrs. John A. Rabbit Go Home

They wound up sailing out of Messina on the U.S. flagged commercial cargo ship named the Salmon P. Chase. To get there they had to take the train from Catania, which they did on September 15th. The Chase was a cargo ship which had been fitted with hospital berthing in the aft sufficient to transport 86 bedridden passengers. It also had berths for up to 120 regular passengers. Jack purchased a first-class berth for Vittoria for $368.00. It had two bunks, but he slept with the rest of the wounded military passengers in order not to make waves. Nevertheless, he spent many pleasant hours with Vittoria in her room.

On September 26th, the Chase departed along with 22 other merchant vessels in a convoy protected from German submarine wolf-packs and long-range bombers by three destroyers and two frigates. Jack wondered if maybe they had a submarine or two hunting enemy subs under the surface. The trip was uneventful, and they docked in Brooklyn, New York, on November 8th. It was cold and both Vittorio and Jack were unprepared. Ditto for all the other passengers who'd been in Africa and Sicily the last two years - or even longer.

By November 11th, Armistice Day, the soldiers whose injuries were mostly healed were sent to Fort Jay on Governor's Island. Jack was in that group. Vittoria found a room in Manhattan leased by the week to single women involved in the war effort. It was small, clean, and cheap, with absolutely no gentlemen callers allowed past the lobby. She took the ferry back and forth to Governor's Island every day to visit Jack while he was there.

Upon arrival at Fort Jay, each serviceman was given a thorough medical examination and counseling to assist him in returning to the civilian workforce. Jack wasn't as good as new, but he wasn't in pain, so within two weeks he charmed them into giving him an honorable discharge; however, he remained on the Army payroll through February 29th, 1944, as a result of unused accrued leave.

He signed out on terminal leave on Wednesday, November 24th. Vittoria and he celebrated Thanksgiving at the Waldorf Astoria for two nights. Then they took the train to Baltimore, to Cincinnati, to Lexington, Kentucky, and thence to Louisa. They arrived on Sunday the 28th.

Jack was thrilled to learn that the new expanded Greyhound Bus Line route extended from South Shore, in Greenup County, Kentucky on the Ohio River at US Highway 23, all the way to Mayking in Letcher County at the Virginia State Line. It paralleled the Ohio River to Ashland, Kentucky, where it paralleled the Big Sandy River along the West Virginia State Line, thence to Louisa, in Lawrence County, to Prestonsburg, to Pikeville, terminating at the southern Kentucky border with Virginia. It was a scenic route that he would like to take one day just for the fun of it, in that he didn't know anyone at either terminus.

They lodged in the Louisa Hotel for three nights. Since it was Sunday, everything was closed. Jack said they had much to do. The most critical thing they needed to do was patronize Ellicott's Mercantile, because they both were in dire need of some winter clothes. Monday morning, they purchased blankets, sheets, pillows, towels, and other sundry items such as two more pots, some dishes and tableware, which Jack hadn't needed being all on his own. He also purchased two cedar chests to ward off moths and to store stuff. Then he paid a young man with a cart to take all these new acquisitions to their room in the hotel.

Next, he went to the Western Union Telegraph Office and got a pocketful of change so he could make a telephone call. He had no idea what it would cost, having never made a telephone call before. He urgently needed to call Woodrow Falstaff, proprietor of Falstaff's General Store at Lonesome Corner, a mile or so from Rabbit Hollow. By the time he had finished talking, he'd deposited $1.05 in silver. It didn't cost as much as he had imagined.

"Falstaff's General Store. Woodrow speaking."

"Woodrow, this is Jack Rabbit. How are you and all the family?"

"My gosh, Jack! What a surprise! We're all just fine. Where are you?"

"I'm in Louisa. The Army discharged me after I got my 3rd Purple Heart and recovered from my last wound. I'm well now. I'm here with my new bride, Vittoria Maria Rabbit, née Bianchi. She's from Italy."

"Well congratulations! I can't wait to meet her."

"She's anxious to meet you and Gerard and his family, too. I'm guessing Gerard hasn't put in a telephone line during my absence."

"Nope. Nobody has around here. They'd have to put in telephone poles and run a line all the way from here to there, same as to your place. It would cost too much, but even if it was free, they ain't anyone around what could do it. Most of the young men done been drafted or j'ined the service. You might say it's slim pickings in these here parts due to everything going to the war effort.

"Think about this. I ain't had no guns nor ammo to sell for nigh on two years now. It's a good thing you and Gerard stocked up afore you left."

"That's pretty much what I figured would happen. Not surprising that Gerard hasn't got a telephone. Who would he call anyway? Nobody but you has a telephone line. So far as you know, is everything okay with Gerard and his family?"

"Everyone's doin' well. I'll tell him you asked."

"Good. Look, could you go see Gerard for me? Ask if he or Chloe could clean the cobwebs out of my cabin and put in a few victuals for us until we can get settled in and get what we need from you?

"Then, would it be possible for you to pick us up tomorrow? We could meet you at the hotel about noon if that would be okay. We could pick up anything you need from here and have it ready for you when you get here. I know it's a big ask."

"Nope. I'm all stocked up on what's available, but thanks for asking. Be happy to pick you all up. It's much happier for me than when I dropped you off to j'ine the Army."

"Okay, then. Thanks. We've got two trunks filled with stuff I just purchased since we didn't have any winter clothes. It stays hot all the time over there in North Africa and Sicily."

"I bet. Don't fret none. We got you all covered. See you all tomorrow at noon and welcome home, both of you. Bye."

"Bye."

After he hung up, Jack said, "Come on. Let's walk over to the Louisa Post Office. Let's find out what you need to do to start the naturalization process. Might as well get the ball rolling. I know you have to read a bunch of stuff about American government and history and pass a written test. I expect we'll have to go to Lexington to do that, but that'll be a ways down the road."

The postmaster gave Vittoria a form to fill out. She completed it, and then they posted it to the U.S. Immigration & Naturalization Service in Washington, District of Columbia.

The next stop was at Schepler's Jewelry, the only jeweler in town. Gold and silver were at a premium due to everything going towards the war effort, but Mr. Schepler went in the back and found a plain gold wedding band for Vittoria, which he sized down for her. He only charged them $8.00. He told Jack if he could find one in his size, he'd mail him a postcard and let him know.

Jack asked what he had in the way of watches. He said all he had was steel pocket watches which came with a braided leather thong for $2.00. Even though they were steel, they were manufactured by the Ball Watch Company and kept very good time. Jack bought one of them, too. Mr. Schepler set it to the exact second from his antique gold timepiece.

The rest of the day they browsed around, taking in the sights, and generally looking at each other with goo-goo eyes like lovers and newlyweds do.

Tuesday morning, Vittoria said, "Jack, put on your uniform. It's not that cold today. Mr. Falstaff may have several folks waiting for you when we arrive. They'll want to see their returning hero in uniform. You may not have the rest of your medals with you, but you do have the Legion of Merit and the Combat Infantryman's Badge. You have one service stripe on one sleeve and three overseas stripes on the other, not to mention your sergeant stripes. Plus, you have the Honorable Discharge patch on your right breast. Besides, you're still technically in the Army, so show them what a dashing soldier you are.

"I shall wear that beautiful new black and white dress you bought me, and I will wear my medal, too! I want everyone to know how happy I am to live in America and how much I want to become an American citizen."

"Right you are, Mrs. Rabbit. Soon as we get dressed, let's go eat at Good's Restaurant. I'm famished."

Woodrow was fifteen minutes early. He was mesmerized by Vittoria's grace, good looks, and charm. He also thought Jack looked every bit the hero he was. He'd seen the *Stars & Stripes* newspaper photograph of Jack receiving the medal he wore on his chest. He knew it was a great honor. Then he noticed Vittoria's medal and asked, "Gosh! Were you in the Army, too?"

"No. I was part of the Italian Resistance who fought the Nazis. The major who commanded the American Army in Catania awarded me this medal for my service to America."

"Gosh!   That's   a   great   honor   and   distinction. Congratulations."

It was a pleasant 30-minute drive to Woodrow's General Store at Lonesome Corner. The sun was shining brightly, and they were enjoying a mild winter day with temperatures up in the 50s. They went inside, where they were greeted by everyone from the local area. They had prepared a surprise welcome home party, which Vittoria thought might happen. Jack was overwhelmed.

For the next two hours, they celebrated in typical hillbilly fashion. They gorged on fried chicken, country ham, potato salad, deviled eggs, rat cheese, pickles, corn pudding, applesauce, biscuits with butter and jelly, black-eyed peas, vinegar, tomato, cucumber, and onion salad, apple pie, cold milk, iced tea, and of course, tin cups of white lightning.

A four-man band with a guitarist, banjo player, fiddler, and mandolin player played one Bluegrass hillbilly song after another. Quite a few well-wishers started to tap their toes and clap their hands. Some even began dancing. Jack was beside himself with gratitude. Vittoria was thrilled with the warm welcome by everyone. She wept tears of joy off and on during the celebration. Everyone was so nice to her, and they didn't even know her. She knew right off this was where she wanted to live out the rest of her days.

Gerard and Chloe and their three kids, Amos (9), Willow (8), and Flo(rence) (6), all embraced Vittoria as if they had chosen her personally to be Jack's wife and their aunt. They were all so full of life and welcoming. Everyone was joyful. Chloe told Vittoria to come visit with her anytime she just needed a little female companionship.

Finally, it was time for Vittoria to get acquainted with her new home, so Woodrow drove her, Jack, and Chloe over so they could settle in. On the way, Chloe pointed to her house to show Vittoria just how close they were.

When they arrived, Chloe opened the door for Vittoria, which had no exterior lock - just a cross bar to be inserted from the inside like the partisan cabin in Sicily. In fact, Jack's cabin looked to be very similar to that cabin, except for being a mite smaller, plus it had more windows - two each front and back, and one on each side.

Vittoria saw how spic and span it was - she could even smell the Pine Sol cleanser - and that it was well-stocked with canned goods and other victuals, which must have just been purchased for them. She said, "Oh Chloe, I know Jack asked Mr. Falstaff to ask if you could clean out the cobwebs before we arrived, but you way outdid yourself. You must let me repay you in kind."

"You will. I know you will. There will be days when the young'uns will get underfoot too much and then I'll shoo them over here to pester you. We can sew quilts together and churn butter and all sorts of things. I'm thrilled to have you as my sister-in-law and as my next-door neighbor (next-door being a half mile away)."

"Me, too."

By then Jack and Woodrow had finished carrying in their belongings and it was time for Chloe and Woodrow to return to their own domiciles. They said their goodbyes, and Jack and Vittoria were left alone. After all the hullabaloo, it seemed so quiet. She hardly had time to take in her surroundings because everything had happened in such a rush.

Jack said, "Well, I hope you're not disappointed. I told you it wasn't much. We do have a beautiful view on all sides of the cabin, but the best is from the verandah looking out over the vale and Rabbit Creek down below. Most folks call it Troublesome Creek, because it has been known to flood a time or two, but on our property, we like to call it Rabbit Creek. We just missed the autumn colors, but they'll be back next year."

She ran into his arms and embraced him mightily, shedding more tears of happiness. She said, "It's just like you described it. What a picturesque place to live and we don't have to fear Nazi or Fascist murderers anymore. I love it."

He replied, "That we don't.

"Well, you can see that I heat via the fireplace, but I also heat and cook on the stove. I didn't have a stove at first. I also have a hand pump over the sink and a galvanized tub for washing. The privy is out back. I have neither electricity nor telephone and we probably won't be able to acquire either until after the war ends. I do have two kerosene lamps, and I'll buy another if you think we need it. I hang my wet clothes on an outside line to dry, although in winter they freeze first as they dry. I guess I could string another line inside.

"Also, I'm down to $230 from my Army pay, plus the $160 in a cloth sack tucked away in that trunk by the bed. At least I still have three more checks coming in, but I'll have to figure out how I'm going to make a living.

"While I was gone, Gerard tilled up 10 more acres to add to the 20 I had already tilled. I own 160 acres overall, but over a hundred are forested with hardwood trees so we'll never lack for firewood. I don't have a barn per se, but I do have that oversized outbuilding with stalls for four animals but right now I only own one. She's a 9-year-old gray mule named Alice. I also have a redbone hound named Oswald. Gerard's been taking care of them for me while I was gone so we'll walk over and bring them home tomorrow.

"What I'm trying to say is, although I farmed 20 acres which was mostly corn with one acre set aside for a vegetable garden, my income was derived by making moonshine with Gerard. If all I did was farm, we could cover our expenses, but we wouldn't have much left over to purchase any expensive items, such as a tractor or an automobile, even if someone had a good used one for sale. We've always plowed with mules or horses.

"Gerard plowed up that ten acres to raise tobacco and I might could do that because, even though it's hard work, it pays a heck of a lot more than corn. I'll talk to Gerard tomorrow and see if he's still in the moonshine business and if he has enough clientele where I could join him again. If not, I reckon I'll be strictly legitimate, but we'll probably never have much money. So, you see, I have land, but I don't have much money.

"One other thing. We had a moonshine war here in 1920, in which we licked a gang of city slicker bootleggers down from Cincinnati. Killed 'em all. We've never had any trouble after that. My firearms consist of a Remington 12-gauge, double-barrel shotgun that was my pappy's, and a Smith & Wesson .38 caliber revolver I bought from Woodrow. I'll get them back tomorrow from Gerard.

"Anyway, that pretty much brings you up to date. I hope you're not disappointed."

Vittoria leapt up into his arms with still more tears streaming down her cheeks. She said, "Jack, I could never be disappointed with you. You're a good man, a brave man, a simple man, a kind man, and I will always love you. You have all we need. I thought I would never find love, but you found me. I'm the happiest that I've ever been before my whole life."

"Well, what if we have children?"

"Then God will provide. He always does."

They enjoyed a simple supper meal and retired for the night. Vittoria thought she was in Heaven on Earth.

Chapter 15
Reconnecting With Home Sweet Home

The rest of the week passed quietly. Chloe and Gerard left them in peace to get settled in. The way it happened, on Wednesday Gerard said, "I think I'll ride over on Alice and take Oswald with me ta Jack's. It's nigh on ta noon."

Chloe replied, "Gerard, we got to give 'em a little space. You know they's still newlyweds. You recollect what that's like. After we was married we didn't come up fer air fer five days. They'll come around afore long. Besides, we didn't fight in no war or have ta sail across the ocean ta get home. Not on'y that, Jack's still recovering from all his wounds. They done shot him twice. I hope he don't get too vigorous and rip up any stitches."

"Yer right. I'll leave 'em be."

Chloe knew what she was talking about. The solitude was exactly what they needed.

Sunday morning, December 5th, they came up for air. After an early breakfast, they walked over to Gerard's farm. They wanted to stop by before he and the family departed for church.

Chloe asked, "Why don't you all come with us? Vittoria, everyone will want to meet you. I think you'll like it."

Gerard chimed in, "Absolutely! It's no problem. We always take the wagon drawn by my new draft horses, Ichabod and Matilda, sose I can show them off. Jack, you ride your mule. Vittoria, you ride my mule. His name is Walter. Today, Chloe's mule, Wilma, will get the morning off."

"Jack, I know you all came to get your belongings I kept for ya, but ya can pick them up after church."

Chloe added, "Vittoria, after church we'll come back here, and you can help me make dinner. I'm planning to make chicken and dumplings with cornbread and green peas. We'll top it off with bread pudding. What do you say?"

Vittoria looked at Jack and he nodded. She replied, "I can't think of anything I'd rather do. The other things we need to take care of can wait until tomorrow, can't they, Jack?"

"You bet."

That's what they did.

The Holy Ghost Baptist Church was small, just like most buildings in the Rabbit Hollow community. The church was erected in 1855. Putting everything in perspective, in 1944 the population of Lawrence County was only 15,000 souls spread over several hundred mountainous miles, which were connected mostly by backroads and horse paths.

Louisa, the county seat, was truly just a town itself and hardly big enough to be considered a city. With 8,000 citizens, it boasted the largest population of any community within Lawrence County. The area known as Rabbit Hollow, which included Lonesome Corner, only had 31 families spread out over six or eight square miles, except the shape was not square. It was more like the shape of a protozoa situated on an angry red anthill.

Ergo, the Holy Ghost Baptist Church was a rectangular wooden building painted white. It had a tall steeple with a cross on the top. It featured one arched, stained-glass window on the wall behind the pulpit depicting Christ on the Cross. Besides the pulpit, it had five rows of benches divided by an aisle down the middle. The pews on each side could seat eight worshippers, for a total of 80. They never had that many attendees except at weddings and funerals.

The privies were located behind the church.

The church cemetery was on a knoll to the left of the building. It boasted a larger population than the church itself, home to more than a hundred markers of all types for the dearly departed.

The pastor was Brother Enos M. Byrd, age 52. He was assisted by his wife, Sister Maybelle Marie, age 47. They were both scarecrow thin. He was tall and bald. She was short with piercing blue eyes and a hawk nose. To many, they both appeared to be constipated all the time due to their dour countenances, but in fact, looks can be deceiving because they were just the opposite. Both were gentlefolk.

A chalkboard on the wall listed the songs they would sing by page number in the pew hymnals, which were copyrighted in 1883. It also listed passages in the Bible by book, chapter, and verse, from which Brother Byrd would be preaching that morning. The hymnals were furnished, but each family was responsible for bringing its own King James Bible. As of this date, the church did not have an organ, but all the members hoped to acquire one someday.

Vittoria was somewhat surprised when they approached the church. She only counted three automobiles. However, there were eight buckboards and six saddled equines, both horse and mule, who were tethered to the various hitching posts. In many ways, Lonesome Corner was like Speranza - rural, small, and years behind the times. Vittoria was learning firsthand that not all of America was bustling and modern like New York City, which she had recently experienced for herself. Nevertheless, Eastern Kentucky was beautiful, peaceful, and charming in its own Southern backwoods' way.

Brother Byrd was a captivating orator, and well-versed. He was modest and humble - anything but an angry Bible-thumper. He had a gentle aura surrounding him and was much adored by his parishioners. He and Sister Maybelle Marie jointly introduced Vittoria to the church family, giving her a warm welcome. They also welcomed Jack back home from the war. The service lasted an hour and a half, after which they returned to Gerard and Chloe's cabin. The kids changed clothes and went out to play. Chloe and Vittoria prepared dinner. Gerard lit his pipe and Jack lit up a cigar. Then the men got down to business.

Jack said, "Thank you all for the reception yesterday, cleaning up my cabin, and for stocking us up with victuals. How much do I owe you? I know it was you all who provided the bounty of victuals.

"Not a thin dime, Cuz. Shame on you for even asking. Blood's thicker than water. You'd a done the same for us if'n things was reversed.

"Now you're back home in one piece, praise the Lord, what do ya aim ta do?"

"That's a darn good question. I don't know. I have enough money stashed away to get me through the winter and spring, but I need to decide soon how to earn a living. You got any suggestions? Is moonshining still an option?"

"I'm glad ya finally got around ta askin'. Ya know, not much has changed here in this neck of the Commonwealth. We still got 120 counties and 100 of 'em are still dry. Alcohol is legal in most areas of the country, but not here. Louisa is 18 long miles away and folks here still have a thirst for distilled spirits. My price has gone up to a buck fifty a quart because sugar's hard ta come by and it costs more ta get. Fortunately, I can still get it from

Ellicott's Mercantile most of the time.

"Now my rig has six barrels, sose I don't have ta cook as often. Even so, sometimes when I'd like ta cook, I cain't get the sugar. I still grow the corn ta make into mash, and whatever I don't need I sell, but there's a passel of corn farmers around here, sose it's a sorry way ta try ta make a living ta raise a fambly.

"So . . . . since you was away, I started growing a little tabaccy because there's a lot more money ta be made, but ya gotta get a permit from Uncle Sam ta grow it. They allow you so many acres and I'm allowed five. I grow a sixth acre on the sly and make it inta chaw. I sell that on the black market sose Uncle Sam won't find out I growed a little extre. So far, he ain't never sent nobody around here ta check on me. Besides, I'm just small potatoes.

"I will tell ya raising tabaccy is hard work and will consume most of your time until ya take it ta market in the fall. Not only that, you'll need ta build a tabaccy barn to season the leaf for when ya harvest it. If'n ya want ta try your hand at that, I'll he'p ya build it. Prob'ly cost a hunnert bucks in lumber and nails ta build one just like mine. Not only that, I'll hire ya back ta make moonshine at the same 60-40 split. We'll have ta up production and sales, but I don't think that'll be too hard.

"What do ya say?"

"Thanks, Cousin. I'm all in. I'll be ready to start on Tuesday. Fortunately, I've got enough cash stashed away to erect a tobacco barn. I'll need you to line me up to get the tobacco permit. Guess I might have to wait a bit to buy Vittoria a washing machine."

"Not ta worry. Slim Willy Arbuckle is selling out and moving ta Louisville ta go work in one of them factories - Ford, as I recall, makin' Army trucks. Anyway, they's having an auction on Thursday. Bet ya could get one for no more'n 15 bucks. We're planning ta go anyway ta see if there's something we might like."

"Great. We'll go too. Also, I need to get Vittoria a mule and tack."

"Probably get that at the auction, too. Slim Willy's got several nice ones ta choose from."

"Boy! Wouldn't that be nice? One stop shopping."

"Hey. When ya all get ready ta go home, don't forget ta take your duffle bag and box of medals and guns and whatever else ya left here."

"Thanks for reminding me. I've felt naked without having a gun within reach."

Business concluded, they uncorked a bottle of moonshine and sipped on it until dinner. Afterwards, Gerard carried Vittoria and Jack's belongings home in his wagon. Jack rode Alice. Oswald trotted along beside him.

What? Gerard even sneaked in a wooden box containing six quarts of mountain elixir to hold them over. He was always generous to a fault.

Everything was going to work out.

On Monday, Jack borrowed Chloe's mule, Wilma. He took Vittoria all around Rabbit Hollow past Lonesome Corner. She was impressed with the clarity and clean taste of the water from Troublesome Creek which ran through their property.

Jack couldn't help but boast. He said, "All our water flows over limestone rocks, which gives us a fresh, crisp taste for our moonshine. Not many places abound with water this pure. It has absolutely no bitterness or muddy or metallic taste."

On Tuesday, Jack went back to work with Gerard. They took inventory, counting 119 quarts, and immediately began a new batch of mash. They filled all six barrels with ground corn, sugar, water, and a little yeast, covering the barrels with wooden tops to help begin the fermenting process.

On Wednesday, they made moonshine deliveries, selling 26 quarts, netting $39. Jack had no intention of taking his cut of $23.40 since he hadn't helped with the distilling process on this batch of whiskey, but Gerard insisted. He was that kind of guy.

On Thursday they went with Gerard and family to the Arbuckle auction. Sure enough, they bought a Sears & Roebuck wringer washer for $10; a red 6-year-old she-mule named Sassy for $19; tack for $11; a third rocking chair for $6; and bedding for $3. Jack also bought six boxes of Peters brand 12-gauge shotgun shells - three in number 6 shot, two in number 1, and one in number 7 ½, each with 25 shells per box for $3, for a grand total of $51. The 6's were for small game like rabbits (perish the thought) or squirrels. The 1s were for waterfowl like ducks and geese, and the 7 ½'s were for doves and quail. Vittoria fell head over heels in love with Sassy and rode her all the way home with a smile plastered all across her face. It was a great day.

On Thursday they rode over to Falstaff's General Store and purchased two quarts of milk, two dozen eggs, and of course, the *Courier Journal* newspaper. Vittoria said, "Jack, if you buy me a cow and some baby chicks, we can get our own milk and eggs." That prompted Jack to buy some wood and chicken wire to build a hen house and a fence around it to keep the foxes and raccoons out. He would purchase the chicks after it was built.

He also asked Woodrow how long it would take to get the lumber from Louisa to build a barn. The answer was about a week, COD (cash on delivery). Jack said he needed to check with Gerard first to figure out how much he would need.

Jack and Gerard checked on the still every day to see if the mash was ready to distill. Jack built his chicken coop. Vittoria bought two dozen chicks from Woodrow for a dime apiece. She already knew maybe half of them would perish before they started laying eggs. She also spent some time every day with Chloe sewing patches to make a quilt.

On Friday, Jack went hunting. He shot a six-point buck. They had over 70 pounds of meat after he butchered it. Jack gave half to Chloe and kept the rest.

On Saturday, Vittoria said, "Jack, this is December 11th. Christmas is two weeks away. We need a Christmas tree. Also, what would you like Santa Claus to bring you?"

He replied, "Gosh! I've never had a Christmas tree before in all my years. What would we use for decorations?"

"Don't you fret about that. Chloe and the kids and I are planning to make some. You just get me a nice tree and set it up right over there" (pointing to some empty space next to the door).

"Done."

"You still haven't said what you want."

"Well, I could use another pair of long-handle drawers and some wool socks. It's getting cold out there."

"Okay, I'll ask Santa Claus to bring you some since you've been a good boy all year."

"What about you?"

"I need some leather dress gloves and a heavy winter dress. I wear size 6 and I like green. I saw one in Chloe's Sears & Roebuck catalogue. Also, we're eating dinner on Christmas Day with Chloe. See if you can scare up a turkey a day or two before then."

"I'll keep that in mind and see what I can do."

Saturday was a busy one for Jack and Gerard. They checked on the mash and determined it would be ready to distill tomorrow but decided to wait until Monday because of the Sabbath. They loaded the wagon with 60 bottles of hootch and made the rounds delivering it. They should have packed 80! Folks were loading up for the holidays!

They stopped by Woodrow's where they ordered and paid for the Christmas gifts for their families. Woodrow's wife, Clarabelle, said she would wrap the gifts in colorful tissue paper and put them in a box for them until they were ready to pick them up.

Then they sat down with Woodrow and calculated the cost for everything Jack needed to build a tobacco barn. It turned out to be $111, which included delivery charges straight to his cabin. Jack ponied up the moolah and Woodrow phoned the lumberyard. Delivery would be on Tuesday, December 21st assuming the weather didn't get nasty.

On the way back to Gerard's cabin, they stopped by Harry Butler's farm where Jack purchased a two-year-old milk cow for $8.25. Finally, on the way back home they each cut down a small pine tree and trimmed them up so they would be symmetrical.

It was nearly dusk by the time Jack walked through his front door. First thing he did was introduce Vittoria to her new cow. She named it Esther. She fed it and put it in a stall next to Alice and Sassy. Then she noticed the Christmas tree. Of course, it had to be set up before they could eat their supper! 'No rest for the weary and the wicked don't need none.'

Sunday was church.

Monday and Tuesday were distilling days. They netted 51 gallons of shine.

Wednesday Jack and Gerard made their rounds. They sold 78 quarts of white lightning.

Thursday the temperature dropped to 20 degrees, and it snowed all day long. They got eight inches. Jack spent the day cutting and stacking firewood. Vittoria spend most of the day inside after milking Esther (morning and evening), cleaning, soaking and cooking pinto beans seasoned with country ham for supper, knitting (a sweater for Jack), and reading her family Bible (in Italian) while she rocked in her rocking chair. That night Jack livened up the evening by picking on his banjo. He needed the practice after being away from it during his time in the Army.

This pretty much summed up their lives during the winter. Life was simple. They worked hard. It was peaceful, especially for Vittoria after living through nearly five years of war. They were both happy and content. They had no trouble sleeping at night.

Chapter 16

Christmas Day, 1944

Today was the most festive day of the year for folks in Lawrence County. Jack and Vittoria got up early and did their chores so they could celebrate. Jack had bagged two turkeys which Vittoria had cleaned. Then they put their packages in a large poke and rode over to Gerard's. Jack had even purchased a dozen oranges as a treat, which they brought along too.

Chloe had already begun preparing things for the big meal, and the cabin was toasty warm. She made the children wait until after Jack and Vittoria arrived to open their presents. Finally, after all the adults had a cup of coffee and the young'uns had their special treat of hot chocolate, it was time to open gifts. The children went first.

Amos, aged 9, got a Barlow pocketknife. It came with a metal ring at the top to attach a woven, leather tether to fasten to the slit in the bib of his overalls so he wouldn't lose it. Gerard made a dandy one for it and handed it to him after he unwrapped his present.

Willow, aged 8, received a comb, brush, and handheld mirror set. She also received four colorful hair ribbons. She was all smiles. She asked Aunt Vittoria if she would fix her hair as soon as she opened up the package. Of course, Aunt Vittoria was happy to comply.

Flo, aged 6, tore her package open and found a Raggedy Ann doll. She lit up as bright as the North Star.

Chloe got a heavy wool, blue shawl with fringe along the

border to help her stay warm during the cold months.

Gerard got a brown fedora hat to replace his old, disreputable one. He said it was so nice he was afeared to put it on because he might get it dirty.

Aunt Vittoria got the winter weight green dress she wanted from the Sears & Roebuck catalogue. It fit like it had been made just for her. She rushed to the bedroom and changed clothes so she could model it for everyone. She also got a pair of leather dress gloves.

Uncle Jack got a red cotton union suit with a trap door in the back and a gray pair of wool socks. He was pleased, but the children laughed 'til they cried. They thought it was a terrible thing to get for Christmas.

When the kiddos thought open presents time was all over, Aunt Vittoria passed out a small package for each child.

Flo received a coloring book and an 8-pack of jumbo-size crayons for young children.

Willow received a book of paper dolls.

Amos got a pocket-size cloth sack with a drawstring containing a dozen colorful marbles and a taw (larger marble for shooting, referred to as a log roller in these parts).

They were all pleased as punch.

It was a festive birthday gathering for the Baby Jesus.

Jack and Vittoria departed a little before dusk to feed the animals and keep the fire going. The weather was overcast, like it was threatening to snow again, and the temperature was 25 degrees according to the thermometer on the verandah (for which Jack had to light a match to read.)

They weren't that hungry after all they had eaten, but nevertheless, Vittoria baked a small batch of biscuits to go with some country ham and a pot of hot tea for supper. They topped it off with an orange.

After supper and washing the dishes, Vittoria sat in her rocker in her nightgown and robe, covered with a lap blanket. Jack sat across from her in his rocker still fully dressed, smoking a cigar and sipping on some of Gerard's elixir. (He was still dressed because he always checked around the curtilage before he retired for the night.)

After several minutes without conversation, Vittoria asked, "Jack, if I asked you something really personal, something private that you've kept tucked away for years, never telling another soul, would you answer me truthfully?"

"Goodness sakes! What brought this on?"

"It doesn't matter. Would you tell me the truth or not?"

"You know I would. What do you want to know?"

"Here goes. Have you ever heard of a man named Mohan?"

"Mohan? Have I talked in my sleep?"

"If you love me, just answer the question. Yes or no?"

"Yes, but it was a long time ago. I met him once and never saw him again. Why do you ask?"

"Tell me about him. I want to know."

"It was nothing bad, but you wouldn't believe me even if I told you. I'm not ashamed of it, but it might drive you away from me if I told you. That's why I never spoke of it to anyone. You could call it a secret for which I have no understanding - just unanswered questions."

"Jack, I love you way too much to ever leave you no matter what, even if you cheated on me. Tell me this secret so it doesn't become a wall between us, like a trust issue."

"Geez, Louise. This is difficult to explain, but before I do, you must promise me first that you will never utter a word about this to anyone. What I'm about to say does not comport with my understanding of the universe, but nevertheless it's true and actually happened."

"Jack, you have my solemn oath."

"Okay.

"Well, I met Mohan in West Texas many years ago by happenstance. Truth is, I'm a little foggy on this, and I'm not actually sure how long ago it was. He was an Apache shaman of some sort. Very powerful. Something like the mythical British legend Merlin, I suppose, except this isn't a myth. Are you sure you really want to hear this? I'm afraid you will disavow me forever. It's hard to swallow."

"I promise I won't. Please continue."

"Well, if you must know, I came into this world as a jackrabbit - a four-legged, furry, grass-eating creature with long ears, as ridiculous as that may sound. Hence my name, Jack Rabbit. My universe was an acre-sized patch in West Texas in the middle of nowhere. Political boundaries were beyond my comprehension back in those days. Mostly, my biggest concern was trying to avoid the prowling coyotes - that and meat-hungry Apache Indians.

"Understand now? Who on Earth would ever believe this? If this hadn't happened to me, I wouldn't believe it. It sounds crazy because it is.

"Anyway, I was browsing for fresh shoots of grass when I first saw Mohan. He was in some sort of mystic trance alongside a mountain where I happened to be. Seeing an Apache Indian was nothing new to me. Like I said, we shared the same patch of ground. At the same time, they couldn't be trusted not to kill and eat me anymore than the coyotes could.

"So, I heard a sound and looked up. I noticed a few rocks which had started falling from the top of the mountain, bouncing along in Mohan's direction and mine too, for that matter. Then I saw a huge boulder toppling down. Fortunately, I had noticed the entrance to a cave, or perhaps a large crevice in the rocks, right in front of me but behind Mohan. Besides, he was elsewhere in his mind and didn't hear or perceive the peril we were both in. I warned him with a loud screech and hopped into the cave as fast as I could go. It was the most un-rabbit-like noise and the loudest sound I had ever uttered. That's when he noticed me and the landslide and dashed inside right behind me just in the nick of time.

"This is where things really got weird. It turns out that he credited me with saving his life - me, a lowly rabbit! Can you imagine? Not only that, get this! In fact, the only language I ever knew was rabbit, but he knew it too like it was his native tongue and we were able to have an extensive conversation.

"If you think that sounds crazy, the rest is even crazier.

"Mohan built a fire and did some kind of dance and chanted something unintelligible to me. It was mesmerizing. Then he threw some magic dust or something in my face and I fell into a trance - a deep sleep. In fact, I think he might have too. Anyway, when I came to, he said I was a changeling now, his gift to me for saving his life and I would live forever so long as I didn't eat papaya fruit or go to Easter Island. I had no earthly idea what a papaya was, nor had I ever heard of Easter Island. Suffice it to say, I've followed his instructions and done neither.

"I was in utter disbelief so to prove his point, he told me to imagine that I was an Apache warrior, and to go look at my reflection in the creek. I did and sure enough, I saw myself just like an Apache warrior. I recognized my face as a human!

"That's about it. That's everything I know about Mohan. I never saw him again. However, I did learn how to change myself from one being to another, and now I'm quite good at it. I've been everything from a cactus to a rattlesnake to an eagle to a sparrow to a man. I like being a human the best.

"How old am I you ask? I have no idea. My memory sometimes fails me. This much I do know. I have a passion for current events and history. Not exactly sure what precipitated my undying allegiance to the United States of America other than to say I was born here, and I love it with all my heart, just like I love you. Anyway, my earliest, very foggy memory as a human is as a child right here where we live. I told you about my sibling, Phoebe. You know my parents are both dead. They died in a house fire while I was gone during the last war.

"I don't remember enlisting in the Army during the Great War, but I do remember fighting in the trenches as a private in the 1st Division. It was a bloody business, but the Allies finally began winning after America joined the war. I knew more about current events than most of the folks around me, but I knew nothing of the American war strategy at the time as a lowly private. In that regard I was no more knowledgeable than the uneducated soldier standing next to me.

"I don't recall nearly being blown to pieces by an artillery round just before the Armistice. I do know I was hospitalized for a long time and that I had amnesia. It's pretty much a blank until I woke up here, close to Troublesome Creek, wearing a doughboy uniform. That was back in 1920. The rest of what I know came from documents I had in my possession or what Cousin Gerard told me. The name on all my documents identifies me as John Archibald Rabbit.

"So . . . that's it. That's my secret. Now you know. Please don't ask me to change into a mouse for you right now so I can prove my story to you. However, I would like to know why you asked me about Mohan."

"Well, there are two reasons. My first inkling about you was when you were able to do that extensive reconnaissance of the Nazi compound in such a short amount of time. Even so, that wouldn't have given you away had I never met Mohan."

"What?"

"That's right. I'm a changeling, too. I was born a roadrunner in southern New Mexico. I hunted birds, small rodents, lizards and other reptiles for my supper. I'm not sure how old I am either. I didn't have a name, at least not one that would be recognizable to a human. One day just after sunrise, I was running all over the place, jumping fences, looking under creosote bushes, in the crevices of rocks, behind boulders, searching for something besides field mice to eat for breakfast. I was tired of eating mice.

"I was focused so much on finding food that I wasn't paying attention to where I was going. Like you, I had no boundaries. What I saw first was a medium-size rattlesnake slithering slowly along the desert. He was probably searching for food too, or so I thought. I hadn't eaten snake in a while, and it got my mouth to watering for something different. Suddenly, he slithered behind a low bluff at high speed, and I lost sight of him, so I kicked it in high gear. When I rounded the bluff, I saw where the snake was going.

An old Indian was just rising from his blanket, and his back was towards the snake. This snake must have been one of the man-haters because he sped up, homing in on the old Indian for a strike, even though the Indian had done him no harm. He didn't even know the snake was there!

"Heck, I had no differences with the Indians. In many ways they seem to like road runners, and perhaps even respect us. They make jewelry images of us with silver and turquoise which they wear or sell to the American tourists. Roadrunners are woven into their culture.

"So besides making a meal out of that snake, I wanted to save the Indian from certain death. I got there just in time to seize the snake by its neck. I shook it as hard as I could until I was absolutely certain it was dead. The Indian watched me do it with eyes as large as goose eggs.

"Then he bowed to me and spoke and surprisingly I could understand him. He said his name was Mohan and that he was an Apache medicine man. He thanked me profusely for saving his life. He asked if I had planned to eat that snake.

"I replied that I was. Then he asked if I had ever eaten a roasted snake. I said I had not. Then he said it tasted very good and that he would roast it if I would share it with him. I agreed, so he commenced to gather some brush and dead branches and then he skinned and roasted it.

"We ate, and I savored every bite because I had never before tasted cooked meat. It was delicious. While we were eating, he made a comment that it was gratifying to eat the flesh of a mortal enemy.

"Afterwards, he said he had something special for me if I had a little more time to visit with him. Why not? I was sated and it wasn't like I had anyplace I needed to be, so said yes. Then he built up the fire. While he was doing this, he told me my name was Victoria, because I was victorious over my enemies. Then he began to chant and dance just like he did with you. I was spellbound. Suddenly he threw a magic powder on me from a pouch on his waist, and I fell asleep.

"When I awoke, he asked how I felt. I said OKAY, but maybe a little woozy. He said that was normal after the ceremony he had just conducted. Then he asked if I could be anything I wanted to be, what would I choose? I said I wanted to be a puma. You know, a mountain lion. He said for me to close my eyes and imagine that I was a mountain lion, so I did. Then he told me to open my eyes.

"When I did, I was this gorgeous, sleek puma with green eyes. I was amazed. Then he told me to close my eyes again and to imagine I was a human. When I opened my eyes, I could tell I was as beautiful as Cinderella. That's when he told me I was a changeling and that I could be anything I wanted to be whenever I wanted. He also said I would live forever, and the rest of that stuff you mentioned about papaya and Easter Island. That was the last I saw of him. Poof! He disappeared just like that.

"Eventually, one day when I was a human, I went to the Free Public Library in Alamogordo and began reading books about different countries and cultures. I became fascinated with Italy, so I took myself there, first as an eagle, then as a whale, and eventually as a seagull. I wound up in Gela as the daughter of Giovanni and Isabella Bianchi.

"You know the rest. I fell head over heels in love with you and I knew right away that I wanted to spend the rest of my life with you. I too, thought I would never be able to tell anyone the rest of my story, not even you, until I surmised that we both might be changelings.

"What do you make if that, Mr. Rabbit?"

"I'm overwhelmed. I'm ecstatic. We truly are soulmates, Mrs. Victoria Rabbit. I love you with all my heart. I'm exactly where I want to be with you by my side."

"There's one more thing I need to tell you."

"Which is . . . .?"

"I think we're having a baby. Remember those wild nights at the Waldorf Astoria? I missed my menstrual cycle. I think I'm pregnant. If I'm right, the baby will arrive in August. Don't tell anyone until I'm sure. Now we really have a lot to do before then."

Jack rushed over and took her in his arms. Tears of joy were streaming down his cheeks. All he could say was, "Thank you, Jesus" over and over again.

End of story, but would the child be a changeling, too? I wonder.

Acknowledgements

The Jack Rabbit concept is the brainstorm of several brilliant individuals within our publishing environment.

Bruce Moran
Larry Cavanagh
Jeff and Jacki Lovell
Bob Doerr
Linda and Don Brewer
Jessica and Corby Tate
James Thompson
Each of our fantastic Jack Rabbit Fiction Team Writers.

Join me for another
White Glove Fiction adventure
staring Jack Rabbit

ABOUT THE AUTHOR

Earl Snort is the nom de plume of a retired law enforcement officer with more than 42 years' experience toting a badge and a gun. Before that, he served in the armed forces.

He and his wife have been married for 53 years. They reside in the South. They have one son, also a career law enforcement officer, and two grandchildren.

This is the author's tenth foray into the world of writing fiction. After a lifetime of writing non-fiction to document investigations of true crime, he decided to try his hand in make believe.

He hopes you enjoy the yarn.

September 2025

Regarding the tombstone, it reads, "This site May 23, 1934 Clyde Barrow and Bonnie Parker were killed by enforcement officers." It's located near Arcadia in Bienville Parish, Louisiana.

Erected by
Bienville Parish Police Jury

The Lawrence County Moonshine War

Author: Earl Snort
Paper Back: 9781648831782
eBook: 9781648831256
Number of pages: 200
Publication Date: 2022

This is a tale of a changeling shortly after these powers were bestowed upon him. Jack, who began life as a rabbit, fell asleep in arid West Texas shortly after wishing he had a home someplace else in a more temperate climate. When he awoke, he was a young man in a forest glen in such a place. He got exactly what he wished for! The problem was, he was wearing an Army uniform and he did not know his location. He didn't even know which century it was! Jack was suffering from a serious case of amnesia.

He soon learned that the year was 1920 and that he had been slumbering on his own property in Eastern Kentucky. He was re-introduced to his cousin, Gerard, whom he did not recognize, yet with whom he had maintained a best-friend relationship since childhood. Gerard also introduced Jack into his moonshine business during these, the early days of Prohibition. Before long, Jack found himself situated between big city gangsters and state investigators.

Lead was flying in the hills of Eastern Kentucky and Jack was in the thick of it.

A Jack Rabbit Novel

Jack Rabbit Goes To War

Author: Earl Snort
Paper Back: 9781648834189
eBook: 9781648834196
Number of pages: 200
Publication Date: 2025

This book is a sequel to my first changeling book, *Jack Rabbit & the Lawrence County Moonshine War*, although it reads like a stand-alone. It takes place from 1941 to 1944 when Jack enlists in the U.S. Army for a second time to do his bit to fight against world dominion by nations determined to conquer the world and enslave the populace worldwide. There was no way he could have anticipated what would happen.

A Jack Rabbit Novel

Making Mountains Out of Molehills
Author: Earl Snort
Publisher: TotalRecall Publications
Paper Back: 9781590954324
Ebook: 9781590956533
Number of pages: 320
Publication Date: 2019

It was 1969. Barlow Adams, age 20, was a recently discharged veteran. He was driving late at night on a lonely stretch of highway in the Trans-Pecos region of Texas. He stopped to render assistance to a motorist with a flat tire. What he stepped into was a vicious attempted rape. He rescued the victim, which catapulted him into an appointment as a deputy sheriff.

Along the way he encounters an enchanting woman who will change his life forever. In addition, he will be confronted by a gang of outlaw bikers who are obsessed with killing him while he is still learning the ropes of becoming a lawman. Will they succeed?

This is the story of a young man in the 1960's, an era which has long been forgotten except for those who lived it.

Barlow Adams Series Book 1

When Dreams Come True ~ Sort Of

Author: Earl Snort
Publisher: TotalRecall Publications
Paper Back: 9781648830006
Ebook: 9781648830013
Number of pages: 320
Publication Date: 2020

The year is 1970. Barlow Adams is a young deputy sheriff in a rural county in the Trans-Pecos region of Texas. He's a rookie still learning the ropes. Up until now, his experience has been limited to working in the jail and performing routine patrol work that is anything but routine when bad men decide to exert themselves in furtherance of their wicked ways.

In recent months, a gang of rustlers had begun to prey on the livestock of unwitting ranchers. The sheriff has decided to stop them cold wherever he finds them. He employs all the limited resources at his disposal to achieve this goal. One of those resources is Deputy Adams, who learns new law enforcement skills in teamwork, criminal investigation, surveillance, and undercover operations.

Barlow also learns something else. The crime may be solved and plans may be hatched to catch the evildoers, but, in the end, there's usually a joker in the woodpile who upsets the applecart and then suddenly Life becomes a free for all.

Barlow Adams Series Book II

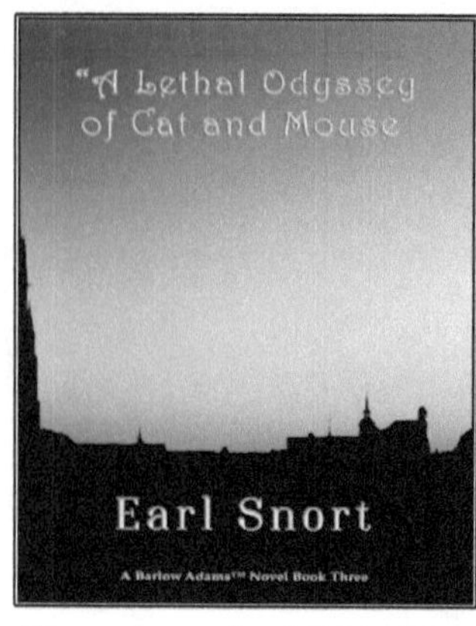

A Lethal Odyssey of Cat and Mouse

Author: Earl Snort
Publisher: TotalRecall Publications
Paper Back: 9781648830785
Ebook: 9781648830792
Number of pages: 320
Publication Date: 2021

The year is 1971. Barlow Adams is a young deputy sheriff in a rural county in the Trans-Pecos region of Texas. After two years of instruction, he completed the Texas Police Officers Standard Training Course, and now he is fully certified as a law enforcement officer. As important as that is, something even more important is about to take place.

Barlow and Sarah, his fiancée, are about to be married.

They don't know it yet, but a depraved outlaw biker Barlow arrested two years ago has decided to stalk and murder Barlow and Sarah while they are on their honeymoon. The outlaw biker isn't operating on his own. He recruits criminals as savage as he is to pull off his barbarous scheme.

By the time law enforcement learns of the plot, the newlyweds have already departed. Until, and unless, they call home, there is no way to warn them.

Tick Tock.

Barlow Adams Series Book III

Evil Lurks in the Darkness
Even When Strong Men Stand Watch
Author: Earl Snort
Paper Back: 9781648831782
eBook: 9781648831799
Number of pages: 306
Publication Date: 2022

The year is 1972. Quayle County, located in the Trans-Pecos region of Texas, has seen an uptick of illegal alien smuggling from across the Rio Grande. The alien smugglers are determined and violent. The Border Patrol is overwhelmed with greater numbers of human trafficking cases in other areas, and therefore is unable to assist. Illegal aliens and Americans are dying alike. The small sheriff's office and the local population are left to their own devices to resolve this crisis.

Once again, Sheriff Solomon Pratt, Deputy Barlow Adams, Deputy Slick Oldman, retired Deputy Archie Willis, plus the new rookie, Deputy E.M. Gillespie, and the rest of the staff on the Quayle County Sheriff's Office rise to the occasion to vanquish the threat.

Barlow Adams Series Book IV

Thicker Than Blood
Murder, Hide & Go Seek Texas Style
Author: Earl Snort
Publisher: TotalRecall Publications
Paper Back: 9781648832567
Ebook: 9781648832574
Number of pages: 312
Publication Date: 2023

The year is 1973. A four-man crew of stick-up artists has been on a rampage in South Texas along the Rio Grande corridor from El Paso to Laredo. One day they stick up the bank and liquor store in Mosby in Quayle County, killing one person and severely wounding another. Mosby is a small town in a large county, with only 3,000 souls and very little crime. Deputies Slick Oldman and Barlow Adams are tasked to locate and arrest the murderers.

Barlow Adams Series Book V

Cleaning Out A Snake Pit,
Before the Wheels Fall Off
Author: Earl Snort
Publisher: TotalRecall Publications
Paper Back: 9781648832765
Ebook: 9781648832772
Number of pages: 356
Publication Date: 2024

It's 1974. Deputy Barlow Adams is on patrol in Quayle County, Texas, late at night. He initiates a traffic stop on a speeding truck. It screeches to a halt, and both occupants bail out, flourishing firearms. A gunfight ensues. One is killed and the other is wounded. A search of the truck reveals 60 kilograms of high-quality marijuana known as Oaxacan Highland Gold, or OHG for short. This leads to Deputy Slick Oldman and Barlow Adams being temporarily assigned to a DEA Task Force in El Paso. The stakes are high and the drug smugglers are deadly.

Barlow Adams Series Book VI

When The Wind Blows Take Head

Author: Earl Snort
Paper Back: 9781648833960
eBook: 9781648833977
Number of pages: 300
Publication Date: 2025

The year is 2003. The setting is the Mississippi Gulf Coast, where Marvin Barnett is a 53-year-old federal agent. A dear friend, Abner Ladner, was just elected sheriff in a South Louisiana parish, and he wants Marvin to be his chief deputy. Marvin accepts, and retires from the Feds.

January 1st begins the new life for Marvin and his wife. He quickly learns that local law enforcement is up close and personal with the public, because every problem is a local problem first. The Feds can pick and choose their battles and they do. All the leftovers belong to the sheriff's office. It can get real messy, real fast. Marvin decided he wouldn't want it any other way.

A Chief Deputy Barnett™ Novel Book One

Random Thoughts
In Case I Don't Make It
Author: Earl Snort
Publisher: TotalRecall Publications
Paper Back: 9781648832789
eBook: 9781648832796
Number of pages: 356
Publication Date: 2024

The year is 1973. Retired police officer Chester Sinclair has a dire situation. Twice within three weeks, unknown subject(s) have tried to kill him. In an effort to determine whom, he reviews 38 years of his police daily notebooks. He comes up with several possibles, but by doing so, he plows up some old ground which had been buried deep within the recesses of his mind. This is the tale of an old warrior pursued by long vanquished evildoers seeking revenge.

Stand Alone Title